RENAISSANCE BEAR

ISBN-13 (e-book): 978-1-83557-037-1
ISBN-13 (print): 978-1-83557-038-8

Cover Artist: Malice & Mayhem Book Covers

RENAISSANCE BEAR

RENAISSANCE SHIFTERS
BOOK THREE

MURPHY LAWLESS

a miz kit production

THE BLACK KNIGHT

THE SKY above burned hot and clear and blue, afternoon heat pounding into the tourney grounds. The knight's horse trembled with impatience, knowing its moment lay just ahead of it: in seconds, they would burst through the gates and pound through the arena— the lists, as a jousting arena was called—to meet their opponent in battle.

The crowd around them was already frenzied: excited voices cheering, toy lights spinning crazily and kazoos buzzing, all kinds of noise-makers that the horse ignored effortlessly. It *lived* for this: the knight had fallen in love with jousting originally because the horses were so obviously thrilled to participate.

Right now, the beast obviously sensed the knight's own impatience. It turned its head to put its nose on their knee, blowing one reassuring huff that spilled warmth through the seams of their armor. It worked: the knight chuckled, patted the horse's shoulder, and relaxed.

Just in time: the gates opened and with a surge of power, the horse leaped forward, thundering down the tilt barrier toward the other knight, a fighter garbed in plate armor. The air scented of hot metal and rising dust and horses, and it was wonderful.

The impact of slamming together, lance to lance, rattled the knight's teeth, as it always did. But the deep grey burnished armor they wore, almost black, absorbed the worst of it, and there was never any danger of falling off the horse. Their opponent weathered the first tilt equally well, and they nodded at each other as they returned to their starting points.

Screams of anticipation rose from the crowd now, a chant of *Black Knight! Black Knight! Black Knight!* thundering toward the sky. There were some who cheered for the other knight, but everyone was here for the Black Knight today, waiting to see if they would win this tourney, as they'd won five others already this year. Through the cries of *Black Knight!* a few also called out the name they'd bestowed on the mysterious knight: *Lord Edward!*

It wasn't the name Edward would have chosen, but being likened to the famous commander who had borne the nickname 'the Black Prince' wasn't something to lose sleep over, either. If the people liked it, so be it: that was Edward's take.

Edward met his opponent in battle again, crashing together at speed, and this time the other knight wobbled badly. Not quite unhorsed, but not well-seated anymore, either. As they rode back, Edward lifted a hand in question: *surrender?*

His opponent shook his head once. Edward nodded in return, patting the horse's shoulder again as they returned for the final time to their starting places. "We've got this."

The horse exhaled again, sounding disdainful. It had never doubted the outcome.

Neither had the shrieking, gleeful audience, whose phones were out to record the final clash, and whose voices were full of the fun and excitement of an afternoon out at the faire. It had been centuries since real knights had jousted for honor, battle, or prizes, but as the horse leaped into motion again, every bone-shaking step felt incredibly real to the participants.

It took a certain set of the shoulder to knock an opponent off their horse, and it didn't always work. Today, though, it did: the other knight took the blow fully, and for a glorious heartbeat seemed to dangle there on the end of the splintering lance, silver armor outlined in sky blue as his horse ran out from under him. Then gravity did its job, and the other knight crashed to the ground in a terrible rattle of metal and earth colliding.

Edward pulled the horse around, gently, and lifted a shattered lance to the sky as if it could absorb the audience's cheers. Grinning beneath the visor, Edward approached the stands and the faire royalty. This was the biggest faire tournament the knight had ever taken part in, with an entire court of 'royalty,' and an arena that held hundreds of spectators. Winning was more than a feather in his helm. It made Edward the uncontested champion for the faire circuit that year. It was also an automatic invite to any jousting tournaments at any Renaissance faires over the next eighteen months.

A beaming princess bent to place her favor Edward's in hand as the king asked what they always did at these events: "Will you not remove your helm, and show us the face of our hero, good sir knight?"

Edward indicated the answer was no with one shake of his head, as always. In response, a groaning cheer rocked the lists. The Black Knight's fans were torn on whether their hero should unmask or not, but Edward had been the faceless Black Knight for nearly five years now. The anonymity was part of the fun. Everyone knew it would take relatively little effort to learn the knight's true identity, but so far, most fair-goers preferred the mystery.

Edward lifted the princess's favor—the only prize the knight ever accepted—and rode away to the cheers and applause of the people. With a pause to shake hands with and appreciate the grooms who took over the horse care once the jousting was done, the knight worked through crowds toward the exit—sometimes stopping to silently sign autographs, but more often simply slipping away before the jousting audience got free of the lists.

It only took a little while to leave the fairgrounds, though walking across what felt like endless miles of parking lot under the sun and in full plate mail armor was probably Edward's least favorite part of the entire performance. After fifteen minutes of sweaty walking, the knight reached the motorhome that served as his base of operations for the faires and climbed inside, finally pulling his helm off in the air-conditioned interior.

A face identical to the knight's own looked up from lounging across the three-seat couch that tucked along one side of the motorhome. "Lo!" she cried. "Cometh Lord Edward, the Black Knight, hero of the realm! Also so, so stinky, oh my god, armor and summer do not go well together, let's get that stuff off you and air it out before I actually die of the smell."

"Thank you. Thank you, Jasmine, that's the nicest thing anybody's ever said to me. Help, get me out of this stuff."

Jasmine, grinning, started helping take the plate mail off, and as the last pieces came off, said, "There we go. Edward is disposed of. Did you win?"

Alissandra Capellas collapsed sweatily on the floor and grinned up at her twin sister. "Of course I won. I'm the Black Knight."

CHAPTER 1

A YEAR OR SO LATER

"Dude, you cannot joust. *I* joust. *You* swan around with a lute and beguile the ladies into drinking at the pub while I swing my sword and seduce them!"

Jon Torben's slightly younger brother, Laurie, had been making this argument for at least half an hour. It was true: normally, Laurie did most of the fighting at the annual Renaissance Faire that they'd been going to since they were kids. He was dressed to fight now, in fact. His long hair was tied back in a very practical braid, and his usual Faire garb of leggings and a tunic with a gorgeous teal coat had been put aside for the leather armor that he used for the on-foot sword fights. He looked like a man prepared to defend his lady's honor.

All except for the crutches and the badly-wrenched right knee that required a decidedly non-Renaissancey medical brace. Jon, for the fourth time in the half hour, gestured at his brother's brace. "Yeah, but you can't fight like that, Laur, and you *can* play the flute. So this summer you can be the roguish charmer at the pub while I knock some heads together."

Laurie dropped his voice. "You know I'm fine, Jon."

"What I *know* is that fifteen people saw you blow your knee out this morning and four of them carried you to the medical unit where they heard you being diagnosed with a torn meniscus, which means you're benched for six weeks, bro."

Laurie, furiously, said, "My knee is *fine*! Or it will be as soon as I can get home and—" He broke off, not wanting to say *shift* aloud, because while Renaissance, Colorado had more than its fair share of people who could transform back and forth from an animal form, discretion was still the better part of valor.

Which was exactly why Laurie couldn't go home, shift, and come back tomorrow miraculously healed. Only really, *really* bad injuries couldn't be fixed with a few shifts back and forth. Which was great...*if* nobody had seen the shifter get hurt.

Jon dropped his voice, too, sympathetic but also knowing he was right. "I know, bro, but a ton of people saw you go down and everybody else is gossiping about it. You're screwed, man. There's nothing you can do about this one."

"I'll tell people it wasn't as bad as we thought it was!"

"*Four people* had to carry you to the medical unit,

Laurie! Look, I get it, I do! It sucks! But man, it's my turn to fight!"

Laurie, sullenly, said, "You don't have the armor for it."

Jon gave him a Look. "We fit in all the same clothes."

That was also true: they were eighteen months apart in age, about half an inch apart in height, and of similar breadth in shoulder, waist and hip. Half the faire attendees thought they were twins, a belief neither of them disabused anybody of. Jon's long hair was darker blonde than his brother's, and his voice was a solid octave deeper, but people often didn't notice those things, and had a difficult time telling the two youngest Torben brothers apart.

It was considerably less difficult when one of them had a brace on his leg, though. "Besides, what are you going to do?" Jon asked with a pointy grin. "You can't chase me if I knock you over and steal your stuff and go fight in your place."

"You wouldn't!" Laurie did a credible look of injury and horror, but he knew perfectly well that Jon would. That was brothers for you.

"You don't want to let the Torben name down, do you?" Jon crooked his fingers, demanding Laurie's leather tunic.

Laurie deflated and put his crutches aside so he could pull the leather tunic off. "It's not the Torben name at Faire," he mumbled into the clothes as he pulled them off and threw them at his brother. One of the tavern wenches whistled. Laurie brightened, pausing to flex as Jon laughed and caught the top as it flew at him. The faire was only just getting started this year, and the Thunder Bear Brewery's pub was opening for the first time in about an hour. They'd gotten the tents up and the rustic wooden seating laid out yesterday, and had brought in the bars, beers, barrels and bites that morning.

And Laurie, showing off for one of the bar maids, had twisted wrong as he lifted a barrel. Everybody within ten feet had heard the horrid *pop* from his knee, and everybody in a three-tent radius had heard his shriek and seen his collapse. It had not been a subtle kind of injury.

Jon really did feel sorry for him, but there was no point in both of them manning the pub when one could be out fighting. It *used* to be that they'd switch, one day and then another, and then one week and another, until it had gradually turned into one summer and another, only Laurie somehow kept being the 'one summer' guy while Jon worked the pub every year. It was way past being Jon's turn. He would have been happier if it hadn't taken Laurie blowing his knee out to get his chance, but at this point, he'd take it.

"I'm going to sign up for the fight slots, bro. You want me to get you a turkey leg from Sampson's?" Jon asked as a peace offering.

Laurie's pout worked wonders on girls, but made Jon want to pull his brother's lower lip over his head. Still, Laurie mumbled, "Yeah, please," through the pout, and Jon knocked his shoulder against Laurie's as he headed out.

The main gates weren't quite open yet, and

although Jon loved the relentless busy-ness of the faire, he thought he loved the hours just before opening even more. The air vibrated with enthusiasm and everybody was in a good mood, looking forward to the crazy bustle of the first evening. People had new costumes, called 'garb' at the faire, and were ready to show it off. Tonight, after the gates closed again, there would be a fantastic party for the faire workers, a huge celebration of being back together and doing something they loved.

Tomorrow everybody would be hung over, and by the middle of next week, weariness would already be starting to settle in, with a month of Faire still ahead of them. But the first night was just about perfect, in Jon's estimation. He scuffed through sweet-scented sawdust paths, waving greetings at friends he hadn't seen in a year or sometimes more, and breathed in the rich pungency of mulled wine over there, roasted turkey legs back there, cotton candy from farther down the fairgrounds. Pretty soon it would smell like sweat and sunblock, too, but right now it was perfect.

The fighting grounds were awesome: a field in three parts, the largest of which was the jousting run. Signups were being held at the sword fighting ring, and there were already a couple of faire workers there, sharing grins at their own enthusiasm. One of them waved and yelled, "Hey, Laur! I thought you got hurt!" before realizing he was the Other Torben Brother, and rearranged their faces to try to hide their surprise. "Jon!"

"Yeah, Laurie's out for the count so it's me this year.

Good to see you, Dale." Jon bumped fists with the skinny fighter, who looked like a strong breeze would knock him over and who—according to Laurie—hit like a rhinoceros.

Not an actual rhino. Not in the way Jon and Laurie were bears. Dale was a true human. So were most of the other faire workers who had shown up early to get their names into the fight rosters. There were plenty of spots already taken: Jon knew a number of people who were basically professional jousters and blade fighters, who took priority in the lists because they put on a good show. The rest of the slots would be filled by tomorrow afternoon, all by people—like Jon—who wanted to make a name for themselves in the fights.

Dale grinned at him as they finished filling out the paperwork. "May the best man win, eh?"

"Loser buys the drinks at Thunder Bear," Jon replied, grinning in return, and stopped for a turkey leg on his way back to help Laurie open the pub as fairegoers began flooding in.

THE NEXT AFTERNOON, Jon was in the fight ring, working hard to kick butt and take names in the qualifying rounds.

The weather was flawless, a blue sky broken only by the western mountains that rose up over his home town; the eastern horizon went on forever, though in the fighting ring the air was clouded by dust that he and his opponent, a big man, had kicked up. The other guy had size on him, and had used that size to knock Jon on his ass. But he didn't have speed, or the secret strength of a shifter, although it would be cheating to use that.

It's not cheating, Jon's bear said. *Survival is all that matters.*

The bear, Jon thought, was a *leeeeettle* more hard-core than he was. It had never quite come to terms with the idea that Jon lived a pretty cushy life and *chose* to fight, instead of *having* to.

And for the moment, that was just fine, because he loved having the bear cheer him on too. Sweaty, grinning, convinced he could take his opponent down in the final few seconds, Jon staggered to his feet and gave an appreciative roar as somebody dumped a bottle of water over him, cooling him under the summer sun. An equally appreciative roar went up, mostly from the women in the crowd, although since he was wearing a metal helm because it was the one piece of real armor they had to have for the 'unarmored' fights, it wasn't like they were getting a really great show. Still, Jon wasn't one to dismiss an enthusiastic audience's cheers, or fail to play into them. He shook his wet head, lion-like—

Bear-like, his bear said, offended.

A rather vivid image of a fat bear shaking river water off popped into Jon's head. It just really wasn't as elegant as a lion tossing its thick mane.

His bear stared hard at him.

The last thing Jon needed was an argument with the bear. That could distract him from the last bout of the fight, and it would be embarrassing to go back to Laurie a loser after making all that fuss about fighting. He conceded, *Bear-like,* and the bear, satisfied and even smug, went back to being enthusiastic about knocking somebody around.

The other guy was on the far side of their fighting ring now, both of them heaving for breath but ready to go for the winning blow. Knowing it would appeal to the crowd, Jon let out a shout and ran toward his opponent, dragging his sword through the dust like he was some kind of anime character. People laughed and cheered while his opponent sneered.

It did *look* very vulnerable, Jon knew that. That was the idea. But he was strong, even without the bear strength, and bringing the blade up and around for a killer blow was incredibly theatrical. The audience liked theatrics even more than they liked the actual win.

But we wanna win! his bear shouted.

Jon, who happened to agree, swung the sword up, kicking dust along with it. He spun, hearing the crowd's cheer rising toward a crescendo. He shot a quick glance over his shoulder, half to see where his opponent was, half to see a flash of grins and raised fists from the gathering, so he could really appreciate how much they were about to love him.

A vividly green gaze met his. Just a glimpse, in the middle of his dramatic athletics. A vividly green gaze in a heart-shaped face, with black curls piled up around her head. A strong nose, a full mouth, wide bladed cheekbones, a flush of pink on golden skin. A long slender neck with an emerald jewel at her throat, and wonderful collarbones displayed by the elegant square-cut neckline of a gown that proclaimed her a lady of rank in the Faire. She was utterly, fabulously gorgeous.

*Our **mate**,* his bear gasped, and Jon, enthralled by her jade eyes, completely forgot he was in a fight. He missed his opponent entirely, and took a hit to the ribs so hard that he collapsed into the dust, heaving for air and trying not to barf as the audience screamed their appreciation of his defeat.

CHAPTER 2

THE LITTLER GUY in the sword fight, Alissandra thought, was the most *gorgeous* man she'd ever seen. Even sweaty and half-hidden beneath a metal helmet, he was one hundred percent fully *hot*. Long, dark blonde hair tied back in a braid that fell between his shoulder blades, deep dark brown eyes, great cheekbones highlighted by the shadows of the helmet, a full mouth pulled into a beautiful smile…he was absolute perfection. And 'littler' was a laugh, too: the other guy was positively huge, because Mr Gorgeous there had to be solidly over six feet in height.

Or he was up until he caught a sword to the belly so hard he doubled over. Alissandra's last glimpse of him was through the milling crowd as he lay on the ground, clutching his gut, grey-faced and wheezing.

Handsome, but not the hero she was looking for. Definitely not one she would be facing in battle, incognito, later. Not if he lost in the qualifying rounds of the unarmored fights. Which was too bad. Alis wouldn't half mind crossing swords with Mr Gorgeous, in both a very literal sense and a highly metaphorical one. But as things stood, she would have to offer her favors elsewhere.

Literally. Not in an eyebrow-waggling way, or a *doing somebody a favor* way. Any time her sister was up for it, Alis played two parts at the faires they attended: the Black Knight, and a lady of the court. Otherwise Alis only played the Black Knight, because the quick changes between armor and fancy, Renaissance-style 'garb' were too difficult.

But Jasmine was up for it this time, so for the next week, Alis would be alternating between playing the role of a lady of the court and armoring up for the lists. 'Lady Alessandra' was a member of the Red Court whose primary duty was bestowing chivalric favors upon her favorite knights. When Alis had to be at the lists, fighting, Jasmine would take over the role of 'Lady Alessandra,' but otherwise, Alis's story for the Faire was to choose a knight, be wooed, and as part of the huge final weekend, participate in a theatrical production of a wedding with the knight she'd chosen.

Sadly, Mr Gorgeous clearly wasn't going to make the cut, which was a shame. It would have been nice to have an actually hot and sexy Faire boyfriend. Alis gave a dramatic sigh that ended in a giggle at herself as she worked her way out of the sword-fight-watching crowd. As the Black Knight, she didn't have to partici-pate in the early elimination rounds. In fact, she only *had* to show up for the semi-finals.

That, though, wasn't any fun at all.

She broke free of the crowd unexpectedly, almost tripping over her own feet when there were suddenly no more people to push through. For a small-town faire, the attendance was spectacular, but Alis guessed that was what they got for hosting a Renaissance fair in a town *called* Renaissance. Not only did the name beg for the faire, but the setting was staggeringly pretty. The kind of place a person would like to tuck up under the covers in, and call home. Which Alis felt was a crazy thing for a big-city girl to think, but it turned out small-town Colorado really was stunning.

The fairgrounds were set at the foot of the Rockies, and wound around clumps of sharp-scented pine trees and aspens that somebody'd had the foresight not to clear away entirely. It meant shade on hot sunny days. Alis was sure vendors would like to be set up beneath those trees, but instead, picnic tables and other seating were provided beneath them. That made sense to her: the tents and kiosks were hot, but at least provided their own shade. Having places where people could rest out of the sun was a great idea. Alis had been to way too many faires where there hadn't been any shade at all.

The other thing all the shady places offered was a place to pitch her own changing rooms. This was one of the few things Alis requested, as the Black Knight: somewhere private to don her armor. Some places couldn't accommodate that at all, so she had to reluctantly refuse to attend those faires, because keeping the secret was still half the fun. Eventually she'd have to come clean, and finally get to go to the faires which only used group changing rooms, but for the moment, she only fought at faires who could protect her anonymity.

And the organizers here had offered her a space just behind the arena, more or less beneath the bleachers and backing up to a thick strip of aspen forest. It was perfect, from Alis's point of view. A lot of construction stuff was stored there, boards and planks and a cement mixer, for heaven's sake, as well as huge rolls of canvas protected by tarpaulin wraps, in case any of the booths or tents in the faire were damaged and needed quick repair. Basically, it all looked like a storage area, and nobody was very likely to come looking for a knight's changing booth amidst all the...well, it wasn't really rubble, but that was the word that leaped to Alis's mind, anyway.

She and Jasmine had set up the tent *very* early in the morning on the first day, long before most faire workers arrived. They'd dressed identically, and only one of them at a time had ever been on the fairgrounds, so the fact that there were two of them had almost certainly gone unnoticed. Their little changing space was surprisingly comfortable, which was important, since Jasmine spent a lot of time there, mostly doing her computer programming day job. *Digital nomad,* that was what she called herself. Basically it meant she could work from anywhere, and did.

Alis knocked on a strut next to the tent, announcing herself before she pushed the door flap open. The back side of the tent had a big, fabric-screened window: good for letting air in, bad for seeing through. Jasmine had a water cooler set up along with her computer and a neatly-stacked pile of armor and food. She held a finger up as Alis entered, went back to typing, and worked in silence for another minute or three before closing the computer with a *click!* and smiling brightly at her twin. "How's the faire?"

"Full of beautiful men. Or at least one really pretty one. Lousy fighter, though." Alis had already unzipped her gown and hung it on the small clothes rack by the time Jasmine finished work, and was pulling on the padding that went beneath her armor.

Jasmine laughed and stood to help Alis tie some of the padding in place. She was already dressed in an identical gown to the one Alis had just removed: deep red, with gold trim on the square neckline, and long belled sleeves that almost dragged on the ground. "Not going to win your heart, then?"

"I don't know, he's hot enough that I might forgive him as long as he's got other sword skills, if you know what I mean. You sure you're good in here?"

"I always am." Jasmine had worked out of the RV yesterday, sticking with the air-conditioning while Alis only had the role of Lady Alessandra to play. Today, though, Alis had to armor up, so Jasmine was on site, alternating between her actual day job and playing Alessandra. "Dying for some lemonade, though."

"Well, you can get some as soon as you finish becoming Alessandra." Alis pinned her hair tightly to her head as Jasmine started strapping pieces of armor in place. They had this down to a fine science, one that made the quick-change fun. Jasmine took her necklace off her as Alis finished her hair, and put it around her own neck, basically completing her transformation into Lady Alessandra. It took another few minutes to finish changing Alis into the Black Knight, but as almost always happened, they were giggling with delight as they finished up. Jasmine fished her phone out of one of the dress's non-regulation pockets and they took a selfie, two identical faces beaming back at them from the phone screen.

"Someday," Jasmine said, tucking the phone away again, "someday I'm going to get to post all these pictures and people's head will explode when they finally realize how you've been getting away with it all these years."

Alis snickered. "It helps that it's never occurred to them that 'Lord Edward' might be a woman."

"Or that 'Lady Alessandra' might be two women," Jasmine said cheerfully. "You know you could get your ass handed to you, right?"

This was practically ritual: Jasmine always asked, and Alis always nodded solemnly in return and said, "Not that it matters. The Black Knight is invited to be part of the semi-finals anyway."

"It's good to be the king."

"Knight."

"Whatever!" Jasmine bonked against Alis's armored shoulder, winced, and laughed, which was also basically all part of the ritual. "Anything I should know about being Lady Alessandra today?"

"I don't think so. Oh, except if you flirt with the hot guy, definitely let me know how that goes."

"Ewwwww. Not gonna flirt with your hot guy. Also, how would I know who he was?"

"Obviously he's the one you'd look at and go, 'Oh, Alis would think he's hot' about!"

Jasmine paused. "I want to say there's no way that would work, except we have a long history of being able to do that while not thinking said guy is hot at *all*."

"Twin power," Alis said solemnly. "All right, the armored division qualifiers are coming up and that's my round. Come cheer me on?"

"Do I ever not?"

"Constantly, when you're not here."

"Oh, shut up, you know what I mean." Jasmine gave Alis a fond boot toward the tent door, and Alis stumbled along obligingly, but stopped to put her helm on before leaving. "See you in a few, Lord Edward."

Alis thumped her chest and threw a peace sign as she headed out into the dappled light behind the stands, then found herself grinning as she turned toward the arena's entrance.

She *loved* this. Her stride lengthened, armor clanking as it moved easily with her. It weighed a ton and smelled like a hot engine, but she'd been playing knights in armor since she was a kid and it never, ever got old. 'Lord Edward' had a swagger to his walk that made Alis feel invincible, and the way the helmet narrowed down her line of vision to the fight gave her a focus that still thrilled her, even after doing this for years. She took a long way around, moving into the crowd, not to blend in but so it was less obvious where she'd come from, and stopped for a few pictures on her way to the lists.

Even if she couldn't see them as she approached, the sudden roar of excitement at her arrival would have guided her into the fighting arena. Cheers went up, first a mishmash, then steadying out into, "*Lord! Ed! Ward! Black! Knight!*" that went on as she strode over to collect her sword and shield, then became a thrilled cacophony when she lifted the sword into the air.

She felt *strong*, as a fighter. She'd learned how to take a hit a long time ago, but more importantly, she'd learned how to avoid them. Most of her opponents were men, and she lacked their upper body strength, but she was fast and had thighs that could keep her going forever. If she couldn't beat them with pure skill, Alis was a champion at wearing them down.

The crowd's yells propelled her into the fighting ring, where her opponent held his weaponry with competence, but also sagged, just a little, as Alis entered. Psychological warfare was a hell of a thing, too: plenty of people just didn't want to fight the Black Knight. This guy had lost before the battle even started. Alis slammed her sword and shield together, making a huge noise, and the guy's confidence slipped again. Alis, under her breath, said, "This is gonna be fun," and when the bell rang, rushed her opponent.

It was over so fast he hardly knew what had hit him. Alis knew it had mostly been her reputation, but that was just *fine*. It left her fresher for her next round, and an easy early defeat meant the next person she faced would be just that much more nervous about meeting the Black Knight in battle. She raised her sword again, accepting accolades, and caught a glimpse of Jasmine on the other side of the fence, looking melodramatically swoony over 'Lord Edward.'

"Let me favor you, my lord!" Jasmine cried, waving a handkerchief in the air.

Alis placed her fist over her heart, shook her head slowly, and then raised three fingers into the air, earning a trilling cry of dismay from her ridiculous twin.

"The Black Knight will not accept my favor with fewer than *three* wins to his name!" Jasmine called. "Could any other knight be so noble? Oh, my heart!" She fluttered, and Alis, walking dramatically back to the ranks to await her next fight, fought down a giggle. Jasmine would have to take it down a notch or Alis would end up marrying *herself* at the big wedding production at the end of the faire.

Two more rounds of armored fights took place before it was Alis's turn to go up again, facing the winner of the qualifier that had followed hers. This guy was less cowed by her reputation, but size for size, they were incredibly well matched: he had a bit of reach on her, maybe, but Alis was faster. Half a dozen blows later, she knocked his legs out from under him and demanded a yield by placing her sword over his heart. Then she raised her hand to the sky, lifting two fingers this time, and Jasmine squealed with anticipation at the third win which would allow her to offer 'Lord Edward' her favor.

The third round, almost an hour later, was *worth* it:

her opponent this time, a big man who moved thoughtfully and slowly, spent a lot of time testing her. Long enough that her arm strength began to fail, although she played it up, trying to make herself look weaker. Panting, sweating, enjoying herself throughly, she waited until *his* reflexes were slowing, and finally made an attack at the weakness his tests of *her* had exposed: a tendency to drop his guard when he thought he was out of her noticeably-shorter-than-his reach. She stumbled once, moving a step closer, and lunged beneath the broad sweep of his blade, slamming her own (blunted) tip against the joining of his armor on his sword arm side. As his sword dropped to the ground in a billow of dust, Alis knew that his fingers had gone numb from the hit.

His eyes jerked to hers, sheer astonishment in them, and then he was down, the third defeat of the day by the Black Knight. To the sounds of delighted cheers, Alis offered him a hand up, and they shook, her opponent pulling his helm off to smile crookedly and shake his head. "You're really good."

She inclined her head politely—Lord Edward didn't speak in public if she could help it—and put her fist over her heart again in acknowledgement. Then she went to get her favor from Jasmine, who was yelling and waving the handkerchief like a gleeful idiot. She tied it around Alis's armored biceps, made a show of fluttering and swooning, and finally, reluctantly, allowed herself to be taken away by the rest of the ladies of the court who had joined her at the lists.

Alis, grinning beneath her helm, turned to wave at

her cheering fans, and, to her delight, caught a glimpse of the gorgeous guy from earlier. He was even better-looking out of a helm and padded leather armor than in it: she could see the golden highlights in the looseness of his dark blonde hair, and she swore that in the setting sun those deep brown eyes of his had elements of honey drops in them. He was grinning and cheering along with everyone else, until she thought that for a moment, their eyes actually met and his smile fell away like he'd been hit with a brick.

Oh well, Alis thought with an absolutely ridiculous sense of betrayal, so much for *that* summer romance.

CHAPTER 3

JON'S EYES met the Black Knight's, and his bear said, *Our mate!* with the same gasping delight it had used when Jon had seen the woman in green earlier.

"What *no!* No, that's not—our mate was—we saw her earlier!" Jon actually said that out loud, then nearly swallowed his tongue, hoping no one around him had heard, or at least, noticed. Fortunately the crowd was incredibly loud, still cheering the Black Knight, chants of *Lord! Ed! Ward! Lord! Ed! Ward! Black! Knight!* echoing around them repeatedly.

This is our mate, the bear said with enthusiasm. *We must go meet our mate.*

No, we— Jon looked around frantically, and to his heart-lurching shock, saw the green-clad beauty from before slipping away from the crowd. *There! That's our mate!*

His bear looked back and forth between the Black Knight and the Green-Eyed Woman's disappearing back as she faded into the fairgrounds, then beamed at Jon from inside his head. *Our mate!*

Blood rushed through Jon's ears, sending a wave of dizziness over him. *Our...mate?*

Yes. Our mate is a great fighter, the bear said with considerable admiration. *Fierce and strong. Stronger than all the rest! And beautiful!*

Jon stared blankly toward the Black Knight, who had turned away, and then once more looked after the dark-haired, green-eyed woman who was now invisible with fading light and distance. "Our...mate?"

You have gotten very stupid, his bear informed him airily. *Be quiet and follow our mate.*

But which...?

It didn't matter. The Black Knight had been swept into a crowd of admirers, and the woman was long gone. Jon, still dizzy, staggered away from the fighting ring. He needed to talk to Laurie. He needed to sit down. He needed a *drink*. Not necessarily in that order, but all of those things could be accomplished at the Thunder Bear Tavern, so he staggered that way, trying to order his thoughts.

His *mate*. The bear was certain of it. They'd seen the lady, and she was Jon's mate, and they'd seen the Black Knight, and *he* was Jon's mate, and...

Jon definitely needed a drink.

Not that he was in the habit of drinking through his problems. He thought that for somebody whose family owned a brewery, he probably drank remarkably little. But once in a while, a drink was the only answer to sit and think with. Now, for example. Definitely now.

The sun had just fallen behind the mountains, and the air was getting colder, meaning that although the faire didn't close for another ninety minutes, people were now mostly starting to head *out* instead of *in*. Jon moved against the tide, barely able to put one foot in front of another, much less think very clearly. His mind kept flashing back and forth between the woman in green and the armored knight, unable to…choose?

His bear rolled its eyes. *Why choose?*

Jon made a slightly panicked noise in his throat and surged into the Thunder Bear Tavern, which was still incredibly busy with the First Friday crowd. Patrons sat around the log chairs and tables, drinking local beer and shouting cheerful conversations at each other. A number of faire workers had already drifted in, ready for the after-faire party—the tavern didn't usually close until midnight or one a.m., although technically they could stay open as late as two, and sometimes did at the end of the faire.

"Jon!" Laurie, still in the thigh-to-ankle knee brace, lurched over from behind the bar. "Thank god, it's nuts and I'm slow as hell with this thing, I need help!"

"No, Laur, I'm…I gotta…I need to…" What Jon *wanted* to do was go hide behind the tent with a beer while he stared into the distance, but his brother was right: the tavern was crazy busy. There were enough staff members if they were all in full fighting form, but Laurie's injury really did mean the service was obviously running slow.

And a few months ago their cousin Ashley had taken Jon to task over not treating the pub work as a serious job. She'd been right, too. He and Laurie spent the summers at not just Renaissance's faire, but at other ones around the country, running the tavern and promoting their family's brewery. They'd both gotten in the habit of basically taking the rest of the year off, helping out in a pinch, but not, like...*actively* helping, even when they were scheduled.

Ashley had become the brewpub's manager just before last Thanksgiving, and had been completely fed up with the two youngest Torben brothers by Christmas. She'd ripped Jon a new one, and he'd been trying to do better since.

Which meant that no matter how much he wanted to go hide and try to wrap his mind around his... *mates*...

He could barely even think it. Better to get busy slinging beer and helping his brother out. "I gotcha, Laur."

Laurie said, "Thank God," again, and for a while Jon really was too busy to think. The tavern was their pride and joy, a lot of work but a lot of fun, and Laurie's "Last call!" forty minutes later came as an actual shock to Jon. Then they were crazy busy again, pulling the last drinks for faire attendees, and all at once the remaining patrons were on their feet, heading out with promises to be back later in the faire.

A few minutes after ten, with stars glittering overhead, Jon finally grabbed a beer for himself and went to throw himself on the ground behind the tavern tent. Laurie limped out after him, gesturing accusingly.

"What are you doing? We've got twenty people in there still!"

"They work the faire," Jon said to the stars. "They can wait a few minutes on their beer. Besides, the tavern wenches are covering it. Laurie, I think I might be...bi?"

"Be by what?" Laurie sat down awkwardly on a stump, stretching his injured leg out and glaring at it. "It sucks that I've got to wear the stupid thing all summer. How did the qualifiers go?"

Laurie brightened as he asked the question, and Jon tried to sink into the dirt and expire of embarrassment, admitting, "I lost. I was doing really well, I totally had him, but then...I saw my mate, Laur."

Laurie, in the middle of an 'aw man you *suck*' tirade, sat bolt upright and gaped at him. "What? You what? Here? Your mate? Dude! Holy crap! Congratulations! Mom's gonna flip!"

"Yeah, no, I know, I mean, she lost me the fight," that was with a thin crack of laughter that Laurie echoed much more loudly, "but she was gorgeous, Laurie. I don't know her name, I don't know anything, I just... but then..."

"But then what, dude?"

"I was at the lists later," Jon said faintly, gaze focused hard on the stars above. "I caught a glimpse of her leaving, but I also...the, um. Um. The Black Knight?"

"Yeah, Lord Edward." Laurie's tone turned sulky. "Again, hurting myself totally blows. I was gonna kick that dude's ass."

"Yeah, well, I was watching him fight—he's really good, I don't know if you *would* have kicked his ass—"

"Dude! Whose side are you on here?"

"—bro will you *listen* to me!" Jon sat up, suddenly bubbling with frustration and anger, and Laurie blinked across the darkness in surprise.

"Yeah. Yeah, Jon, sorry. What's wrong?"

"*He's my mate too!*"

Laurie's jaw dropped. He pulled it back up, worked it a couple of times, and emitted a small inquisitive squeak.

Jon slumped. "Yeah, I don't know, that's how I feel about it too. But my bear is super sure."

"Oh, so you meant…you might be *bi*," Laurie said, stunned.

"That's what I said!"

"I know but I thought you meant like beside something! Dude! Holy shit, dude! Have you ever gone for a guy before?"

"No! I mean…no! I mean, you know, David Bowie, but…"

Laurie waved a hand. "Everybody would've gone for David Bowie, he doesn't count. Holy shit, dude. Two mates? I mean…holy shit!"

Jon collapsed backward into the dirt again. "Does that even happen? I don't see why it *wouldn't*, but I don't know, don't I have to move to a hippie community in California for that kind of thing?"

"Nah. There's tons of hippie communities here in Colorado." Laurie grinned at him, but the expression fell away into amazement again, and then concern. "Are you okay with this?"

"I don't know? Yes? I guess? I just thought, you know, I guess I thought if I was bi I'd have known by now? But also I guess maybe it's meeting the right guy? Although God, that's a lot, like… that's a whole *thing*, isn't it? Like, can it be fated mates if you're not sure you want to bang somebody?"

"Yeah, sure, of course, it's not like ace shifters don't find mates," Laurie said with another wave of his hand.

Relief sluiced through Jon. "Yeah, good point. I mean, I'm not saying I wouldn't, I just don't know if I would? And does this mean Lord Edward and the green-eyed woman are also mates? What would have happened if they'd seen each other before I saw either of them?"

"I think you need to drink that beer instead of just lying there next to it," Laurie said firmly. "And I guess if you're all mates then if they'd seen each other first they'd be just as confused as you are about seeing somebody *else* that fate says 'yes' to. Unless they're true humans." He squinted thoughtfully as Jon sat up to drain half his beer. "In which case I guess they'd just be like 'ooh, he's hot, ooh, he's hot too, lookit me hooking up with the two hottest dudes here, go me,' or something. Or, y'know, maybe Lord Edward's not into guys either and the two of you are just meant to totally worship…what's her name?"

"I don't know! I got chopped in half at the end of the sword fight and was trying not to puke while she disappeared into the crowd! I didn't get her name!"

Laurie laughed. "Excellent first impression, dude."

"Oh, shut up." Jon threatened to throw the beer bottle at his brother, but he hadn't finished it yet, so he didn't. Laurie still pretended to fend off the projectile, then scooted around on his stump, trying to make his hurt knee more comfortable as Jon had another drink. "You doing okay?"

"Yeah, it's fine. It hurts, but a couple of shifts and it'll be fine. I just wish half the fair hadn't seen it so I could *not* be stuck with the brace all summer."

"Maybe it was fate," Jon said. "If you didn't get hurt I wouldn't have been at the lists and I never would have seen my mate. Mates...."

Laurie's eyebrows quirked. "Oh. Yeah, well, okay, that makes sense. Fine, I'll stop sulking. I wouldn't want you to miss out on your mates. But you didn't talk to either of them? Not even Lord Edward?"

"I couldn't get through the crowd. He's got a huge fanbase. I knew that, obviously. We've been hearing about him for years. It's just knowing it and *seeing* it are totally different. And honestly I was kind of stunned, so overall I haven't made a great impression on either of them today, I guess."

"Fortunately you've got the entire faire to make up for it."

"Assuming Lord Edward even stays around," Jon said dolefully. "He's been invited to every faire on this side of the Rockies and will probably just head out to another one soon."

"Well, that's not going to happen. Not without you

two getting a chance to connect, anyway," Laurie said firmly. "Fate wouldn't jerk you around like that."

"It did Penny and Ashley!"

"*Ashley*," Laurie pointed out, "had like *three weeks* to talk to Penny when she was first here and just couldn't get up the nerve! You're just gonna have to grab the bull by the horns, dude!"

Bear, Jon's bear said sulkishly.

*Bears don't **have** horns,* Jon said. The bear stared at him, its eyes practically brimming over with tears and its jaw all but trembling, and he groaned. *Fine. Grab the bear by the horns.*

The bear beamed.

Laurie snickered. "Your bear's giving you grief, isn't it?"

"Swear to God if I said I was trying to be quiet as a mouse—"

Bear!

Jon, aloud, said, "Bears aren't notoriously quiet!" and the bear glared at him.

Mice squeak!

"And bears *are* pretty quiet," Laurie added. "For something their size, I mean."

"Now whose side are *you* on?"

"Yours," Laurie said fondly. "Look, finish that beer and let's get back to the tavern. You can play music and brood handsomely and hope that one of your mates comes to admire you."

Jon perked up. "Do you think that'll work?"

"God, no. But you can try." Laurie lurched to his feet, hobbled over to Jon, and offered him a hand up that ended in a quick hug. "Seriously, Jon, it might be overwhelming and unexpected, but congratulations, man. I want you to be happy, you know that, right?"

"Yeah, sure," Jon mumbled into his brother's shoulder. "You just want the rest of us paired up so Mom has other people to ask for grandkids."

"Nah. I know I'm her favorite and she really only wants *me* to have 'em."

"Oh my God, bro, you suck."

Laurie cackled. "Yeah, I know. Now come on, let's get back to work." He limped toward the front of the tavern, and Jon, shaking his head, followed behind. Odds were good that either Lord Edward or the green-eyed woman would show up at the tavern eventually. Most people who worked the faire did, eventually. Although the woman was more likely: Jon knew Lord Edward guarded his identity carefully, and that there was a betting pool of people trying to figure out who he was that ran at the faires he attended. So maybe he wouldn't show up, but the woman probably would. But probably not tonight.

He'd just about convinced himself of that as a handful of the local 'bards' arrived. A cheer arose and one of them waved Jon down. "Come on, get your lute, we need somebody who can play strings better than Charlie here."

Charlie played the banjo better than Jon could ever hope to play anything at all, but he laughed anyway. "And somebody who can sing better than Peter there."

Jon *did* sing better than Peter, but wasn't about to say so as another laugh went up. He went behind the bar counter for his lute, tuned it up while the others argued over what song to start with. He knew from experience they'd still be arguing in forty minutes. Instead of encouraging them, he ducked his head over the lute and struck a few chords before starting in with a chorus that he knew would drag them all in. "*Will ye go, lassie, go?*"

The others—Peter on the fiddle, Charlie on the banjo, Shorty on the bodhrán—lifted their voices in aggravation that he'd made a start, but everybody was all in by the middle of the chorus, and as the little band began to sing, so did the gathered faire workers. Jon bent over his lute, concentrating on the four strings until, several songs later, a soprano rose in a counter harmony to the song. He lifted his head, smiling, and for the third time that day, looked straight into the eyes of a fated mate.

CHAPTER 4

MOST NIGHTS after a battle as the Black Knight, Alis would lose the armor and go back to the RV to collapse dramatically for the rest of the evening. Sometimes Jasmine would carry on playing Lady Alessandra for a few hours, so that her absence wasn't noted post-Black-Knight-fight, but as often as not, both twins would end up giggling over popcorn and watching movies while rehydrating for tomorrow's faire.

That evening, though, as Alis had retreated to their changing room and eyed her gown, Jasmine had given her a wicked grin. "Gonna go find your hot sword boy?"

"And abandon my sister to a boring evening of coding all on her own? Would I do that?"

"Absolutely."

Alis had laughed and hugged Jasmine. "Are you sure that's okay?"

"Well, they tell me it's good for twins to develop

their own personalities and interests, you know. Maybe it's about time we did that."

Alis, an elementary school teacher, stared at her sister, a computer programmer, until Jasmine laughed. "Yeah, okay, maybe we've got that covered. But also maybe I have a hot date I'm not telling you about, but I need you out of the RV for it."

"Do you?" Alis lifted her eyebrows hopefully.

"No. I *do* have a project due on Tuesday and I'm only halfway done with it, so I can't watch movies tonight anyway, so you might as well go look for hot sword boy. Just don't bring him back to the RV."

"He is *extremely* hot," Alis said, "but I can't imagine the disaster of an early-faire hookup that turned out to be lousy and then having to keep seeing the guy for the next week."

"Maybe it'd be great and you'd have a passionate but brief affair to remember when you're old and boring."

Alis squinted at her twin. "Why do I have to get old and boring?"

"Somebody has to, and it's obviously not going to be *me.* Turn around," Jasmine added, since Alis had stopped halfway through getting dressed to argue with her. "I'll zip you up and you can go look for sword boy."

"All right. I'll text in the wildly unlikely event that I won't be home by, I don't know, midnight." Alis turned and let Jazz zip her up while she fixed her own hair to reduce the helmet-head look she was currently sport-ing. Then she turned back to her sister, gesturing at herself. "Will I do?"

"Babe, you're almost as gorgeous as I am, and if

Sword Boy doesn't want to hit it, he's got no taste anyway. I'm gonna tidy up here and then head back to the RV where there's actual air conditioning."

"Thanks, Jazz. You're the best twin anybody could ask for."

"I really am." Jasmine had waved Alis off, and Alis had wandered the faire as it slowly wound down for the night. The 'Red Court,' one of two major factions of actors in the faire, was set up on the east side of the fairgrounds, and was filled with human 'royalty' and courtiers. The Silver Court, to the west, was 'faery' and mostly dressed like they were the elfin lords from the movies, although there were a number of more earthy elves and fairy creatures among them. Throughout the days, the courts had an ongoing rivalry that was part of the fun of participating in the faire as an actor.

The rivalries were played out in human chess games, in the various fighting tournaments, and in half a dozen other scenes that sprang up around the fairgrounds every day. It was all more or less scripted, in the same way professional wrestling was: everybody knew the end game and had certain lines they were supposed to say or things they were supposed to do, but they had some freedom to improvise within that.

Alis was *very* happy to stick to her own specific job of "find a knight, cheer him on" because off the fighting fields, improvisation was not her strong suit. But between and after the scenes they were meant to play, she got to walk around the faire, checking out the booths, chatting with visitors, and taking pictures. Lots and lots of pictures. That was what she loved most about being a member of ren faire casts: talking to the people who came to be whisked into a magical world for a little while, so they could forget about any troubles in their own.

Her thoughts danced back to the guy Jasmine had dubbed Sword Boy. She *could* use him taking her mind off her troubles for a while, maybe. Not that she had any real troubles just then. And not that she'd been kidding when she'd told Jazz that a faire romance gone wrong at the beginning of the season would be a total disaster. Still, he'd been *so* pretty, and Alis couldn't remember the last time a guy had taken up this much space in her brain for more than a minute or two.

"Beer," she told herself firmly, aloud. Beer would be a distraction from Sword Boy, and she'd get to know a bunch of the actors from the Courts if she went over to the tavern after hours. This early in the faire, everybody had a lot of energy and enthusiasm for meeting up with old friends and making new ones. By the third weekend they'd be having hard time making it through the day, never mind hanging out all night, so Alis figured she should take advantage while she could. And a party was definitely going on: she could hear singing and instruments coming from the direction of the tavern.

She saw it had a great setup as she approached: a semi-permanent structure for the back wall and actual bar, with a banner featuring a silhouetted grizzly against a foaming beer mug pinned snugly against the upper wall. Picnic tables, benches, and backless log seats were protected from bugs by fabric screens that fell from the heavy canvas tent roof, and there were fans set up in as out-of-the-way places as they could be, making sure the now-cooling air kept moving.

The musicians—five or six of them, mostly men—had gathered in one corner next to the bar, perched on one of the picnic tables and on log seats that had been dragged around it. A wider circle of tavern patrons had pulled more tables and chairs around to face the band, and for a minute Alis stood at the outskirts, looking at everyone and taking it all in.

Everybody was still in costume: tavern wenches with underbust corsets and low-cut blouses wove through silver-clad elfin lords and velvet-adorned human courtiers. The musicians, men and women alike, wore loose shirts with long billowing sleeves, tucked into or belted over snug-fitting breeches and tall boots. People wore their hair in intricate braids, or cropped anachronistically short, which Alis thought was very sexy when combined with the romantic styles of clothing.

There were men in kilts and women in breeches, beautiful flowing gowns and snug-fitted tunics, corsets and leather, and costumes that were half made up of things bought at a department store but combined with *one* thing that sold them as fantasy Renaissance. Alis loved them all. Someone she knew from the Red Court waved a greeting, and she went into the crowd calling hellos, pausing to order a tankard of ale, and sat down near the musicians. Half the gathering was singing along, which made conversation hard, but she chatted with a couple of people before the musicians struck into a song that made the guy next to her laugh and say, "Not exactly traditional," before Alis recognized it and laughed, too.

"No, but if they can use instrumental Taylor Swift in *Bridgerton*..." She threw her voice high, turning the chorus into a harmonic round up where the fiddle sang high. "My-my-my-my Galway girl, my pretty little Galway girl." Other people joined in, catching the tune as it came back around, and Alis threw herself into the joy of singing until the guy on the lute looked up, his gaze fastening unerringly on hers.

Alis's voice squeaked on a high note and she clapped her hands over her mouth, caught somewhere between laughter and embarrassment. She'd only seen the top of his head for the last several minutes, and yet somehow couldn't believe she hadn't *recognized* him, since even the top of his head was attractive.

Hoo boy, she had a crush. Usually she had to at least talk to a guy before becoming enamored, but Sword Boy Lute Player was stepping into a brand new, undiscovered space for crushing. His hair was still loose, and had mostly been hiding his face as he'd bent over the instrument. That was her excuse for not recognizing him.

Well, that and she'd had exactly two brief glimpses of the guy before now, which wasn't the world's best basis for quick and easy identification. In the tavern's evening light, his brown eyes were completely black, deep and easy to drown in. As she watched, he tucked some of his hair behind his ear, and if she'd thought he was handsome before, now she wanted to giggle. That jawline was good enough to write sonnets about. The awed astonishment in his dark eyes could sustain a girl for a week. The breadth of his shoulders, now that he was straightening up from his lute, practically pushed the musicians around him away. His voice, when he spoke, was deep and melodic. "Laurie, take over."

He shoved his lute to the side like he expected someone to magically appear and claim it. Someone did, actually: another blond limped out from behind the counter, looking so much like the lutist that Alis blinked. After the blink, she could see the other man was a little shorter and his hair was lighter in color, but they almost as identical as she and Jasmine were.

His voice was also lighter. "What? I don't play the lu —" He followed the lutist's line of view to Alis herself and finished his protest with, "*Ooooh,*" which made her feel sort of like maybe they'd been talking about her, or maybe like he just recognized the kind of girl his brother was into.

She assumed they were brothers, anyway. Presumably twins. Which was almost enough to make her leap up and run away, because this kind of thing led to double marriages and cousins who were also each other's aunts and uncles and stuff, and Alis was having none of that.

On the other hand, she was definitely prepared to have some of *that*, where *that* was the lutist, who rose to what had to be a solid six two without once taking his eyes off her. He wore a fitted doublet in honey brown, currently unlaced, as were the laces on the cream-colored shirt he wore beneath it. His breeches were the high-waisted pirate-style breeches, made of a slightly tawnier shade than the doublet. Alis, her attention caught by that high waist and the double rows of matching buttons, was stricken with the almost irresistible urge to start unbuttoning them.

Fortunately he was out of arm's reach, although as he thrust his lute into Laurie's hands, it appeared he had every intention of closing that distance immediately. Which he did, by dint of actually stepping *over* one of the other musicians. A woman, at least. A small woman, sitting on the ground as she played her tin whistle. Still. That was a lot of leg, to step over somebody like that.

And then he was there, a huge masculine presence scenting of beer and wind and sunshine and deodorant, with a sting of sweat in the background, which Alis couldn't blame him for: the faire was hot work. He said, "Hi," in that resonant deep voice of his. "I'm Jon."

"Alis. You got your ass handed to you this afternoon."

Very smooth, she thought: *excellent way to get on a guy's good side. Remind him of his failures. Ten out of ten for pickup lines, Alis.*

"I did. In my defense, it was because I'd just laid eyes on the most beautiful woman I'd ever seen."

To her complete surprise, Alis not only laughed, but blushed, hands rising to cover her cheeks. "Oh, wow. Very good, that *was* smooth."

"'Smooth' suggests it's a line." His full mouth pulled into a wide, crooked smile. "I'm completely serious. You took my breath away."

Alis laughed again, shaking her head. "Pretty sure the big guy with the other sword did that."

Something very strange happened in his eyes, a flickering uncertainty as his gaze suddenly darted around the tavern gathering before coming back to her for a determined smile. "Big guys with swords aren't my usual thing. Beautiful women with dazzling green eyes are. That was beautiful," he added. "The singing. You've got a great voice. Are you a professional?"

"Oh, no, but thanks. And you play the lute. Very ren faire of you."

"I picked it up before I was old enough to realize girls go for the guitar players."

"Surely you can switch hit." Alis didn't know if that was true. She knew next to nothing about stringed instruments.

Big Jon's gaze did that uncertain flicker again before he shook his head, then, like he'd taken a moment to actually hear her, shook it again, harder. "You'd be surprised. I did learn to play the guitar eventually, but it wasn't as easy as I thought it would be after playing the lute for a decade."

"What made you pick it up, then? The lute?" Alis knew they were standing in the middle of a crowd, that music and conversation were going on around him, but as far as she was concerned, there was no one else in the whole world besides herself and Sword Boy Jon the Lute Player. And they were talking about lutes, like they'd spent half a lifetime already getting to know each other on different topics. Without meaning to, she lifted a hand to put her fingertips on Jon's chest, just to make sure he was real.

His big hand covered hers with electrifying warmth, and even Alis's distant awareness of people around them fell away. She'd never felt a touch that seemed so *right,* so comforting and roughly sensual all at the same time. All she wanted was to stand on her toes and kiss this big man.

Without letting herself think about it any more than that, she did.

CHAPTER 5

ALIS'S MOUTH touched Jon's, and the world stopped.

Everything. Everything. The scent of beer in the air, the laughter and the music around him, the faint itch of cooled sweat and the dull ache in his ribs where he'd taken the hit earlier. It all vanished into the press of Alis's lips against his own. She tasted of something sweet, and like traces of sunblock, and like the end of a contented day, and the waking anticipation of a new one.

Her hand, beneath his on his chest, tightened a little, like she was both clinging and making sure of her balance. He dropped his other hand to her waist, supporting her, drawing her in, and she steadied. Her free hand rose into his hair, pulling herself closer, and the soft heat of her mouth opened to his with exploratory hunger. Jon forced himself to remember the world around them, because otherwise the tavern bar was going to get used for things it shouldn't.

They broke apart, both gasping, her green eyes huge and fastened on him as a blush crawled up the blades of her cheekbones. She opened her mouth to speak, and he put his fingertips over her lips, shaking his head. "If you apologize I think I'll cry."

The confused embarrassment in her eyes turned to laughter. "Wouldn't want that, although I like a man who's in touch with his emotions."

Jon could think of *so* many emotions he would like to be in touch with. *Soooo* many emotions. Although possibly those weren't *emotions*, strictly speaking. "I live to serve, my lady."

Alis's enormous green eyes went black with desire and Jon went right back to considering the tavern bar for things it oughtn't be considered for. He was suddenly very aware that they were drawing attention, and as he took a breath to make a suggestion, Alis made it instead: "You wanna get out of here?"

"More than anything I've ever wanted in my life." Except the Black Knight he'd locked eyes with this afternoon, too. Jon pushed that thought out of his mind, because Alis was flawlessly, absurdly gorgeous, and he could hardly stand the idea that he might have to share her in some way. She turned her hand beneath his, captured his fingers in hers, and led him through a tavern crowd that he was now aware were whistling, cheering, and cat-calling. Maeve, on the tin whistle, started playing *Summer Lovin'*, and another cheer went up as Jon fled the tavern in Alis's wake.

Once they broke free of the crowd they were actually running, Jon matching Alis's pace until they were out of the tavern's circle of light, and then farther away, toward one of the copses that littered the fairgrounds. Then they were beneath the trees, suddenly clinging to one another again, holding on as if they'd found a lifeline they hadn't realized they needed. Alis, her face buried in Jon's shoulder, half-sang something, then laughed as he put her back a little, gazing down at her curiously.

"'I think we're alone now,'" she said, and Jon literally couldn't stop himself from singing the next line back at her as she hid her face in her hands and laughed again before smiling up at him.

"I'm going to be singing that for the next week. I'm sorry, I just couldn't help thinking—we were running—"

"Just as fast as we can," he agreed. "Although I have to tell you, lady fair, I can run a hell of a lot faster than that."

"Of course you can. You're a hundred feet tall."

"You're about ninety-nine feet tall yourself." She wasn't, obviously, not any more than Jon himself was a hundred feet tall, but she was only about four inches shorter than he, which was pretty damn tall. Her dark hair, thick with curls, had fallen from the delicate golden headdress that held it tamed in place, and brushed her strong shoulders, so perfectly framed by the square neckline of her crimson gown. "God, you're beautiful."

"Thank you," Alis said with obvious amusement.

"Some days I think you're right. Other days I think I've got a face like a hatchet."

"Man, it can cut me down any time."

Alis burst out laughing and caught his hand again, moving backward until she sat on a picnic table. "That was a pretty good line too. So, hi. I'm Alis Capellas. I do not normally run away with strange men during the first weekend of Faire." She offered her hand, and Jon first shook it, but then bent over it gallantly, not quite brushing his lips against her skin. She still scented of sunblock, and a little of a familiar hot metallic tang.

"Jon Torben. I also don't normally run away with strange men during the first weekend of Faire." He straightened, grinned at her, and backed up to lean on a nearby table himself. "Or women, for that matter. Usually I'm back at the tavern working my ass off, actually."

"You and your…brother?"

"And the rest of the family. Thunder Bear Brewery is ours. It grew out of our parents doing this tavern at faires a million years ago."

"That long, huh?" Alis smiled. "I didn't know people even knew how to brew beer a million years ago. I figured back then people got drunk like those bears on apples."

Jon's bear sat straight up. *She knows we're a bear!*

He laughed, both at the bear and Alis. *No, buddy, I don't think so.* Aloud, he said, "That video of them all getting wrecked on the fermented fruit? Yeah, I think you're right. Beer's newer than getting drunk. You haven't been to the Renaissance faire before, have you?

I'd have remembered seeing you." He grimaced as Alis winced. "*There's* my crappy pickup line, sorry."

"No, that wasn't it. I mean, yes, that's a terrible line, but no, I've never been to *Renaissance's* faire. I teach elementary school and can only do a handful of events a year, so I try to spread them out across the country if I can. This is the first time I've gotten this far west, though."

"Yeah? Where do you hail from, fair lady?" Jon kicked his legs out, crossing them at the ankle as he leaned on the table.

"Maryland."

"Oh! They've got an incredible faire out there!"

"Yeah. My sister and I grew up going to it." Alis's smile lit her from the inside until she practically shone in the darkness. "You've been?"

"Only once, a few years ago. The brewery is expanding its customer base and that's one of the ways we find new markets. The whole company started at this faire," Jon said with a smiling glance back toward the music-filled tavern. "Mom and Dad brewed their first beers here back when the faire was just starting, too, and now it's this whole huge family business. My cousin runs the pub, my oldest brother runs the brewery, I've got another brother out East who's started his own brewpub where he serves it..."

"Wow. How many brothers are there?"

"Four." Jon smiled back at Alis. "I'm the second youngest. You?"

"Just the one sister. That was enough for our parents."

"Are you the younger or older sister?"

He thought Alis looked amused. "Older."

"Is your sister into the whole faire scene?"

She laughed. "Not the way I am, no. She's a computer programmer, mostly. So, hey, did you make it through the early rounds?"

Jon groaned. "You mean, the on-foot sword fighting rounds I was going to walk away with before I ingloriously lost the first fight in the last seconds? Yeah, I did, no thanks to you. I got through on technical points and second slots. Thank God for qualifying rounds, because if that had been a quarterfinal I'd have been screwed."

"Oh, good. I would have felt bad about costing you the advancement, really. No, really!" Alis protested when Jon shot her a skeptical look. She spread her hands, smiling but clearly meaning it. "I'm not in the habit of eliminating my op—" She caught her breath, looking startled, then shook her head. "Well, I'm certainly not in the habit of trying to eliminate fighters by distracting them at the critical moment. That wouldn't be very ladylike of me."

"Does that mean I get an inside track to earning your favor, my lady?" Jon asked hopefully, then faltered, remembering how she'd already given a favor to the Black Knight.

"Oh, no. You have to earn it," Alis said, her tone scolding but teasing. "I'm glad you weren't knocked out, though. I was hoping you'd get the chance to."

"Really? What about the Black Knight?" Jon wished

he hadn't asked as soon as the words came out, but it was too late by then.

Alis's dark eyebrows flew up. "What about the Black Knight?"

"You gave him your favor, earlier! I saw it tied around his arm!" Which, Jon told himself sort of dismally, should be *great*, right? It meant she thought they were both hot, and since fate was pulling him both ways, it presumably meant…well, something good, he guessed.

"Oh." Alis laughed and waved a hand. "I mean, come on. Everybody knows the Black Knight doesn't participate in all of the in-show courting and performances. Every lady at the faire could hang their favor off that shining black armor and we'd still have somebody else at our side for the final show."

"Who do you think he is?" Jon asked idly. "I mean, the dude is famous all over the country at this point—"

Alis snorted. "At Renaissance faires. Ren faire famous."

"It's a kind of famous," Jon said with a smile. "I wouldn't recognize, like, I don't know, watch designer famous, but a watch designer wouldn't recognize ren faire famous, either, so I think we're all allowed our niches."

"Fair. Yeah, okay, that's fair. I guess there's all kinds of famous."

"He's smaller than I expected," Jon added, thinking about the armored knight from earlier. "I thought he'd be…" He gestured at himself, and Alis laughed again.

"Ginormous?"

"No, no, you should meet my older brothers. Laurie and I have nothing on ginormous, compared to Bill or Steve. We got smaller as we went along. But yeah, I figured he'd be a big dude. He's small and fast instead. Not *small*," since the knight had probably been about six feet tall, "but not as big as I expected."

"I imagine it's hard living up to everybody's expectations," Alis murmured, then glanced toward the rowdy tavern. "So that's your day job?"

"Hah. Speaking of expectations? Yeah."

"Oooh." Alis's dark eyebrows rose. "Is that the sound of a discontent younger brother, faced with expectations he doesn't want to fulfill? Will you challenge the heir to the empire for his throne, or join the Merchant Marine to make your own way in the world?"

Jon squinted at her. The half-lit fairgrounds softened her sharp features, but he thought he kind of liked the bright light of day and the hard angles of her cheeks and jaw. Either way, though, she was breathtakingly beautiful, a temptation in green that the night turned to forest-black. "I'm not sure 'Merchant Marine' fits into the same story as an heir to the empire. Although I'm gonna be honest, I'm not actually *sure* what the Merchant Marine is."

"You know what, neither am I." Alis dipped her fingers into a pocket and came up with her phone, its light glowing blue over her face as she did a search and came to Jon's side, leaning on the table beside him. "Oh. Okay, that's way less...I don't know, sexy? Than I thought it was." She turned the phone toward him so he could read it more easily. "Basically it's just a country's merchant ships owned by civilians instead of the Navy."

"Oh. Yeah, that's way less sexy than…" Jon fell silent, trying to pinpoint exactly what he'd thought the Merchant Marine was, then shrugged. "Let's go back to pretending it's whatever kind of romantic thing we vaguely thought it was up until this point."

Alis grinned up at him. "Yeah, let's. But we now know heirs to empires and merchant mariners can definitely exist in the same storyline, so we solved that problem, at least."

"Oh, right. I forgot we were making up my future history here." He glanced back toward the tavern and shook his head. "No, I don't think I'm running away or fighting for the throne, there. Steve definitely wanted to get away, and he did, but what I really love is this." He gestured around the fairgrounds. "Getting out and performing and being the face of the brewery as we expand. I'm not as crazy about the day-to-day running of the business, honestly, but Laurie and I are on the road with the marketing six or seven months a year, so…" He felt his eyebrows draw down, and tried to shake off the thought that bothered him.

Alis's eyebrows rose in turn, though, curiosity in her eyes. "What was that thought?"

"Oh, you're reading my mind already, is that it?"

"Just your face. If I could read your mind I wouldn't have asked what the thought was."

"Hah. Right. Um, I don't know. This is the first year I've gotten to fight in ages—"

"And I almost ruined it for you! I'm sorry!"

Jon shook his head, smiling crookedly at her. "As long as it led to meeting you, it would have been worth it."

"*Another* good line. Damn, mister, you must have all the girls lining up."

"That's more Laurie's gig. So's the fighting. I was just thinking that when we're on the road he's really mostly fighting, not selling the company's wares. I don't know. I guess I kind of hadn't noticed before. Not that he doesn't do his part," he said, feeling weirdly guilty about underselling his brother. "We both work the tavern and everything, it's just…"

It was just that for a lot of the evening meetings, the business aspects that took place around and during the faires, Laurie either had the excuse of a sword fighting tournament to be in, or insisted he'd be fine running the tavern on his own while Jon took the meetings. It had always seemed like a reasonable way to split the work load, but now Jon's viewpoint on that was slipping. "I don't know," he said again. "I just hadn't really noticed it before, I guess."

"And now I've come along and thrown everything into disarray," Alis said, not very apologetically. "Sometimes it's good to get things shaken up a little."

"If we're being totally honest, it wasn't you. Laurie blew his knee out yesterday so he can't fight, and that's probably what really threw the balance off."

Alis managed an expression that was one part pout and one part obviously laughing at herself. "Right, yes, of course. Because it is not, in fact, all about me."

Jon turned to her and deliberately dropped his

already-deep voice into a lower register. "My lady, I'd be delighted to make the whole rest of the faire all about you."

Her eyes widened and she took a short, shallow breath. "Oh wow. Wow, that voice, holy moly. Yeah, I think I like that. Uh. I mean. The faire being all about me? I mean, not all about me, obviously, but—suitor! Courting! You know! The storyline! You! Me! We should do that!" As Jon started to grin at her verbal fumbling, Alis smooshed a hand over her face, pulled it down to leave her expression rueful but less starstruck, and added, "Assuming you can advance in the fight ranks, anyway," in a much dryer tone.

"Do you doubt me?" he asked, mock-injured. "Also, aren't you allowed to just pick a hot bro and hook up with him? In story terms, I mean."

"I like your self-assurance there," she said with a laugh. "And I suppose I am, but people want to see it all acted out, which is easier with the really obvious contestants in the fighting ranks. Although I suppose you could be the farm boy who captures my heart and I marry below myself."

"The Dread Pirate Roberts at your service, madam." Jon swept a bow.

"Buttercup was a farm girl! Westley wasn't below her station!"

"No, but you're not a farm girl," Jon pointed out, gesturing at her lady-of-the-court costume. "And I'm not a member of the court, so if I win your hand, you'll definitely be marrying below yourself."

"Only fictionally," Alis said almost absently. "In real

life I'm a schoolteacher and you own a family business. I think you rank over me in social terms."

"I am *not* starting this relationship that way," Jon said firmly. "Real-life equals or I'm out."

She blinked, then flashed a smile. "Right, yes, obviously. I was just thinking of it in sort of Renaissance-y terms. I'd have to be a man for my ability at scholarship to mean anything, back then. Oh, God, I'm over-thinking this, aren't I? Yes. Equals. I wouldn't take anything else." Her eyebrows rose again. "'Relationship?'"

"Hey, you're the one who kissed me!"

"I didn't know I was starting a whole relationship! But I liked doing it." Alis, still smiling, rose on her toes to kiss him again, soft and sweet, before taking a deep breath and a long step backward. "Impress me at the lists next time, Sword Boy, and we'll see where this goes from there."

Then she disappeared into the night, leaving Jon smiling after her like an idiot.

She is an excellent mate, his bear said happily. *She makes you smile.*

A whole new flare of panic rose in Jon. "She does, but what does that mean about the Black Knight?"

The bear shrugged. *The knight will also make you smile. And will be good for fighting!*

Jon made a sound that could have been a laugh, or could have been a groan. Even he couldn't tell. "You're not supposed to fight with your mate, buddy."

He got a distinct sense of befuddlement from the bear. It said, *But fighting is fun,* yet had a distinct undertone of *no, no, I'm afraid the human is right, fighting is not for mates.* After several seconds in which it obviously tried to wrestle this sticky problem into a satisfactory answer, the bear abruptly curled up in his mind and went to sleep.

Jon chuckled, murmuring, "Yeah, that's a good way to deal with it," and went home to bed himself.

CHAPTER 6

THE LIGHTS WERE STILL on in the RV as Alis approached, so she made no effort to be quiet as she opened the door and climbed in. Jasmine immediately called, "No luck with Sword Boy, then, huh?" and leaned back in her seat to give Alis a cheeky grin.

"Actually so much luck with him. His name's Jon and he's great." Alis scrabbled at her own spine until she found the top of her dress's zipper and shucked it in favor of the shorts and tank top she slept in. "Tall. Handsome. Family owns the brewery that runs the tavern here. He's got a brother who could possibly be his twin." She squinted, trying to remember if she'd asked directly about that, while Jazz made a totally horrified noise.

"No. No, absolutely no way, we are not doing the twins thing, Al. That's too frickin' twee."

"Oh no yeah absolutely you are fully not allowed to fall for his brother. Also I don't think he's your type, like, at *all*, but definitely no even if he is. I saw my guy first." Alis threw herself into the RV's couch and groaned. "Air conditioning, how many ways I love thee… Did you get any work done?"

"Yeah, my brain came back online once I was in the coolth and I got a lot done. What's our schedule tomorrow?"

"Uuuugh, you ask such hard questions." Alice had studied the faire schedule dozens of times and still reached for her phone to make sure she was right before saying, "All right, tomorrow is the next round of armored sword fighting, so that's three hours in the afternoon that you'll be Lady Alessandra. My Sword Boy is in the morning qualifiers and I want to go watch him, but I'll point him out to you in case you want to flutter at him a bit on my behalf while I'm fighting."

"Me flirting with your pretty boy seems super sketch, Al!"

"Yeah, but I can't tell him I'm a twin and I don't want to look like I'm running all hot and cold on him!"

"You could totally tell him you're a twin."

"Then he'd want to know where the real me is when you're being Lady Alessandra!"

Jasmine opened her mouth and shut it again with a click of her teeth. "Dang it. Yeah. All these years of hiding the Black Knight's identity, ruined by a crush? That would be embarrassing. Okay, fine, but only very polite flirting. I'm not getting all touchy-feely or anything."

"Ugh, God, no." Alis full-body shuddered. "Look,

hey, if I hadn't said so, thanks for being my twin. And also for being Lady Alessandra in a pinch."

Jasmine finally shut her computer with a click and gave Alis a fond smile. "You have said it, but you're welcome. On all counts. You know I don't mind, right? Like I absolutely one hundred percent do not want to spend my entire summer sweating through every day at the faires, but I love getting out and doing it for a few hours and then being able to bounce with no guilt."

"I don't think the kids these days say 'bounce,'" Alis informed her.

"That's fine. I," Jasmine said with a sniff, "am a *woman*."

Alis laughed out loud and dragged herself out of the couch to hug her sister. "You're the best, is what you are. Okay. I'm gonna hit the sack. The gates don't open until ten tomorrow, so if you want me to get up early and make breakfast just say the word."

"The word," Jazz said obligingly. "Or we could drive into town and do the diner trick."

"Oh my God. We haven't done that in a long time. Are you hungry enough?"

"Well, I'm not now but I will be in the morning!"

Alis, who hadn't been hungry until they started talking about food, pressed her hand over her tummy as it rumbled. "I guess I will be too. Okay, that'll be fun, but we'll have to go early, because I have to be back, in costume, and at court by ten."

"I get up earlier than you do anyway," Jasmine said patiently. "Worst case scenario, I actually drag you out of bed and shoo you into the diner when I've eaten my fill."

"I'll be up before that!"

"Not if you don't go to sleep now."

"Okay, *Mom*. Hnf." Alis crawled into the bed space above the driver's seat, spent a hazy few minutes reviewing Sword Boy's finest qualities in her mind, and fell asleep while Jasmine was still thumping around.

RENAISSANCE'S BEST-REVIEWED diner turned out to be more or less across the street from the Thunder Bear Brewery. Alis actually squeaked as they passed it on the drive to the diner, and shook her head frantically at Jasmine. "I can't go first after all! I have to get pretty! Sword Boy might be there!"

"First, you already are pretty. Second, this only works if we're dressed and made up identically. Third, I am *starving*, so if you wanna wait, I'm not going to argue." Jasmine, in jeans and a white t-shirt, with her black curls knotted up off her neck, pulled a pair of aviator sunglasses off the dash and slid them on before striking a pose. "How do I look?"

"Exactly like me," Alis said, amused, then shook herself. "Look, if you see a tall, good-looking, dark blonde guy with long hair, do not engage!"

"We've moved on to engagements already?"

To her horror, Alis felt herself blushing. "No! That's not what I meant and you know it!"

"Oh my God." Jasmine pulled her sunglasses off, the better to stare at Alis. "You really like this guy."

Alis put her face in her hands. "I do. I don't know why. I mean, he's cute and nice and has an amazing voice, which is all excellent and everything, but not stupid fluttery gaga-goopy worthy."

"All evidence to the contrary." Jasmine smiled. "I promise not to get engaged, or otherwise engage, until you've at least pointed out the right brother to me. It would be embarrassing if I did a polite flirt with the wrong guy."

"His brother's in a knee brace," Alis remembered. "So if he's not in a knee brace he's probably my guy. Unless there are more of them. Oh. Except he said there were. But he also said his older brothers are ginormous and one of them doesn't live here anymore anyway."

"Yeah? Did you get his ring size and whether he wants kids?"

Alis felt herself turning red again. Jasmine said, "Aw," and snuggled her into a hug before letting go. "Sorry. I won't tease you." She paused. "Much."

"Just go eat. As much as you possibly can," Alis reminded her.

"Yes, Mother, I remember the game." Jasmine climbed out of the RV and went into the diner, leaving Alis to blush again.

Eating a lot was the whole point of the diner trick. It was a silly game they played, where one of them would go stuff themselves silly, and then they'd switch places and the other one would eat just as much. The entire point was just to watch the staff grow increasingly disbelieving as what appeared to be one slim woman ate half a diner's worth of food.

Only one place they'd ever been had figured it out mid-meal. The waitress there had twin sisters herself, and it turned out that Jasmine and Alis *held their forks differently*, a thing neither of them had ever noticed. The waitress, accustomed to paying attention to details so she could tell her sisters apart, *had* noticed. She'd clued in halfway through Jasmine's breakfast, and burst into laughing applause. Alis had ended up coming back into the diner and they'd gotten a picture with the whole staff, everybody grinning like fools. Since then, they'd practiced holding their forks the same way, at least for the purposes of the Diner Trick, and nobody else had caught them.

Alis had the crazy wish for Jon to catch them and to just somehow *know* something was off, which was the most preposterous, romancey thing she'd ever thought. But it seemed almost possible, somehow. She wasn't in the habit of meeting a man and thinking he just felt *right*, but Jon Torben…

…well, it didn't matter how handsome, charming, and right he felt. In ten days Alis would be gone, off to the next tournament, and he would be a sweet summer memory. Maybe, she admitted, maybe even an affair to remember, because she didn't especially want to resist temptation, even though it seemed like this particular temptation might lead to a semi-broken heart.

Alis sighed and tucked herself into the couch so she could watch the diner through the RV's screened window. It hid her from view but let her see when Jasmine—who really could eat a lot—was about done. Their trade-off was a quick easy one: the twin in the diner would realize she'd left her wallet in the RV and would pop out to get the wallet. Then the twin-in-waiting would go in, announce she decided she was still hungry, and order at least as much food as the first one had.

A door slammed somewhere in the parking lot, making Alis flinch upright. Then, to her combined horror and delight, Jon Torben walked past the RV and into the diner, looking all stunningly handsome in the morning sun. His hair was the color of *honey* in the sun, for heaven's sake. Alis wanted to lick it.

The thought made her laugh and mutter, "Hairballs!" out loud. Then she grabbed her phone to text Jasmine: *That's him! Don't engage! No eye contact! But be nice if he sees you! Augh!*

She got one word back: *Chill.*

"I can't chill!" she said, out loud again. "He's too hot to chill!"

Jasmine couldn't possibly have heard her, but twin telepathy really kind of *was* of a thing. Jazz turned from her meal to glare out the window toward Alis and mouthed, "*Chill!*"

Alis whispered, "Chilling," and Jasmine, looking more or less satisfied, went back to her breakfast. At least she kept her gaze down, obviously making an effort to not draw Jon's attention.

Through her screen and the diner's windows, Alis saw Jon see Jasmine, though. He started to smile, but his eyebrows flickered downward into a frown, and he glanced around the diner, visibly confused before approaching Jasmine's table. She glanced up with a polite smile and gestured for him to join her, which made him smile again, though he looked remarkably uncertain as he sat down.

Alis groaned and put her face in her hands for a heartbeat, but looked up again immediately, unable to *not* know what was going on.

Jasmine was stuffing half a pancake into her mouth, that was what was going on. And then some bacon, and then slamming what remained of her orange juice before suddenly looking around as if realizing she didn't have her purse or wallet. She started to stand, obviously explaining, and Jon offered a genuinely sweet smile, shook his head, and reached for his own wallet. Alis wailed, "Oh *no!*"

She was fairly certain Jasmine said the same thing. She certainly had the expression Alis could feel on her own face. Jazz shook her head hard, then bolted from the diner, causing half a dozen patrons and several staff members to look her way, the latter with deep scowls.

Jon stood, visibly apologetic, and waved toward the table as Jasmine threw the RV door open and rushed inside. "He wanted to pay!"

"I can see that!" Alis didn't have to pretend to be every bit as agitated as Jasmine looked. "What did you say to each other?"

"Just hello and I ate really fast and then he tried to pay and go go go!" Jasmine almost shoved Alis out the RV door.

It was barely thirty seconds between the RV and the diner, but Alis was red-faced and sweating as she tore inside. Jon Torben, in the middle of paying for her breakfast, turned back to the door in obvious bewilderment as she yelled, "No! I just forgot my wallet! I'll pay for it! Except I'm still hungry!" and threw herself into the booth Jasmine had vacated.

CHAPTER 7

JON'S BEAR SAID, *Our mate* happily as Alis came racing back into the diner, and Jon howled, *I'm so confused!* inside his own head, directed at the bear.

There is nothing to be confused about, the bear said. *This is our mate.*

But three minutes ago you said she wasn't!

Three minutes ago, she was not, the bear agreed.

But mates don't run hot and cold like that! Jon protested. *Either she is or she isn't!*

She is, his bear proclaimed, and Jon groaned.

He certainly hadn't expected to see Alis in the diner this morning. Even more, he hadn't expected for his bear to dismiss her, completely uninterested. It was like it hadn't even seen her, which was obviously impossible. So he'd said hi, and she'd been…weird. Perfect, of course. Obviously. Amazing. All of that. But also… weird.

It was like the spark had disappeared. Like she didn't want to be here talking to him. As was evidenced by the fact that she'd shoved most of a pancake and some bacon into her mouth so she *couldn't* talk to him, and then followed it with an orange juice chaser before bolting from the diner with some kind of excuse he hadn't quite understood.

Judging from all the plates she'd left behind, though, she'd eaten a ton of food and had run out on the bill. Jon absolutely could not believe that his mate would do such a thing, but he also certainly wasn't going to let the diner eat the cost. He'd offered to pay, and while Connie, the waitress, rang up the bill...

...Alis had come running back in, waving her wallet and yelling about still being hungry. She'd met his eyes with a sort of frantic apology, and...

Zing. The spark was back. His bear sat up and took notice, now Jon, having put his wallet away, sat down across from her with a tentative smile. "Are you, aaaah, are you okay?"

"I'm fine," she said with huge emphasis, like she was willing him to believe it. "This has just been a very weird morning? I am so sorry," she said to Connie as the woman came over to the table uncertainly. "I did say I'd forgotten my wallet but I guess my mouth was full so it was hard to understand me. And I'm absolutely starving. Could I get a short stack of blueberry pancakes, two eggs over medium, sausage, wheat toast, another glass of orange juice and a cup of coffee?"

Connie whispered, "You just...ate..." before pulling together a professional smile. "Yes, of course. Can I get you anything, Jon?"

"Waffles and a cup of coffee, please. I don't think I can match Alis's appetite this morning."

Alis met his eyes for an instant and heat flashed through Jon, sizzling straight down his body to land in his groin. He hadn't meant *that* kind of appetite, but all at once he was absolutely sure he could match it, after all. Alis smiled, slow and sweet, like she knew exactly what Jon was thinking. His bear, enthusiastically, said, *You should mate!*

NOT IN THE DINER!

If the bear's front legs could fold like arms, it would clearly have folded them and sat down in a sulk. *Hmph.*

Connie, who had fortunately missed all that byplay, said, "One waffles, one everything else, coming up," and left the table.

"So, hi," Jon said, still hot under the collar and slightly confused. "Are you sure everything's okay?"

"I am. Honestly. I just…didn't expect to see you this morning? It threw me off?" Alis sounded like she was testing the explanation, though Jon didn't see why: it made perfect sense.

"Yeah, me either. I figured you'd be sticking to the fairgrounds, I guess. I don't know why." He smiled at her. "Maybe because I know everybody in town who does the Faire, so seeing people I only know *from* Faire in town seems all backwards to me."

"Like students seeing their teacher at the grocery store," Alis said, relaxing into a smile of her own. Her stomach rumbled and she put her hand over it, embarrassed. "Sorry. I really am hungry."

"I don't see how that's possible," Jon said with admiration. "I thought me and my brothers ate a lot, but I think you've already put Bill to shame, and he's the biggest of us. And you're coming back for more?"

"Well, you know," Alis said vaguely. "Faire's a lot of work. And I get tired of turkey legs."

Jon laughed. "Spoken like a true Faire regular. The commoners only get them as a novelty, but I'm sick of them by halfway through the season. But my family's pub is right over there—"

As he gestured, Alis nodded. "I saw it on my way in. I love the log cabin look."

"You should see the inside. My cousin's really brought it to life in the last year. Anyway, our house is the next road over, so I come here for breakfast a lot."

"'Our' house?"

"Mom and Dad's. They retired to Arizona a few years ago and Laurie and I are still in the house."

Alis's eyebrows went up. "Wow. That must save on rent. There are moments I consider moving back home because I don't know how else I'll ever save up for a house of my own."

"Hah, yeah. The folks paid off the mortgage before they left, so we basically pay the property taxes and household maintenance and stuff, but yeah. I know how lucky I am. I've been looking at buying, but there hasn't really been a compelling need." Up until now, Jon thought. He would be thrilled to buy a house for Alis to come home to.

Which was getting way ahead of himself. "Do you still live in Maryland?"

"Nooo, um, I'm living in New York now. Teaching

in Syracuse. It's not convenient for coming to faires out West but it's beautiful." Alis glanced toward the windows and the view of the not-so-distant Rockies before smiling back at him. "Different kind of beautiful."

"Oh, Syracuse! That's only a couple hours from where my brother ended up. Do you know Virtue?"

Alis's eyebrows rose and Jon laughed. "New York. Virtue, New York. I am not asking about your personal relationship with virtue."

"My virtue and I are comfortable with our relationship," Alis said with a quick grin, then shook her head. "I don't know it, but—oh, no, wait! Is that the town Zane Bellamy's from? They had that big fashion designer contest a couple years ago and some woman who lived there won. I remember that because she was a school teacher, too."

"Iiiii don't have a clue who Zane Bellamy is, but there's probably only one Virtue, New York, so: yeah? The whole family went out there last year for Steve's wedding. It really is pretty. I mean, upstate New York in general, but Virtue is what I saw the most of. Oh, those look good," Jon added as Connie appeared with plates and plates of food. The waffles she settled in front of him were fluffy and light, though as Connie left again and he tried one, he did lean over the table to murmur, "Don't tell Connie, but my sister-in-law, Steve's new wife, she's a chef and her waffles are *so* much better than these."

"Well, waffles aren't like beer," Alis said. "It's harder to mass-produce them at quality levels." She paused. "I assume. I have no real idea if beer is better in small batches, too."

"It's—different." Jon had to take a bite of waffle to keep himself from launching into a lecture.

"Different how?" Alis, eating her second breakfast with as much gusto as she'd eaten the last bites of her first, gestured with her fork. "I don't want to know everything, but tell me something."

She really was perfect. Jon tried not to beam too idiotically. "Well, okay, so big companies are going for consistency, right? You always want a Budweiser to taste like a Budweiser, and there's this whole process it goes through to maintain that. Smaller breweries like Thunder Bear have more room to play around. We still want our big sellers to be pretty consistent, but if this year's batch is more malty or—" He waved his fork. "Citrusy. Earthy. Whatever. Because of the weather conditions, or something, we can absorb that and feature it instead of considering it a loss. So it's not exactly the same as mass-producing waffles, but it's not all that different in some ways, either."

"Well." Now Alis pointed with her fork, first toward his waffle, then toward the kitchen. "So your sister-in-law is doing, like, super small-batch waffles for the family, maybe. This place is doing large-scale produc-tion like your beers: not everybody is going to get exactly the same quality of waffle but they'll be better than the real mass produced toaster waffles. Right?"

"Yeah, that seems fair." Jon grinned at her. "How do you make talking about beer and waffles so interesting?"

"It's my personal flair." Alis tossed her hair, although it was worn up in a curly, knotted twist that didn't really toss. She looked incredibly cute in jeans and a white t-shirt, a totally classic combination, and she had eaten more food than he would have thought possible even if she *hadn't* been polishing off the last of several plates when he'd arrived. "So will you be at the tavern after the fights this morning?"

"Unless there's somewhere else my lady fair requires me to be, yes. Is there somewhere else?" Jon asked hopefully.

She grinned. "That still depends on how well you do in the fights, so eat up, you'll need your strength. No, seriously, though, there's a set piece around five this afternoon, after the armored fighting, where each lady of the court is supposed to declare her champion for the rest of the faire. If you can be there, I'll choose you."

Jon's heart thumped. "What if I do badly in the lists today?"

"Then my true and trusting faith will see you through the final fights. Do you joust?" she asked, and although it followed the line of conversation, Jon startled.

"No. No, Laurie and I used to want to when we were kids, but Mom saw too many people break arms or legs when they got unhorsed and was like 'nope.' I think she didn't care if we got a broken leg so much as she didn't want to have to deal with us—"

He broke off, suddenly realizing he'd been about to say that their mother didn't want to have to deal with them being forced to *pretend* they were hurt for weeks, in the way Laurie currently had to. But saying that meant explaining why they wouldn't actually be hurt for all that long. Even if he thought Alis was ready to hear that, explaining it in a diner was not a good idea. "...she didn't want to deal with us complaining at her all the time." That wasn't a lie, even if it wasn't the whole truth.

Alis gave a startled laugh. "That seems fair, to be honest. I've broken a couple bones and it's the worst even as an adult. How's your brother's knee, by the way?"

"Speaking of complaining all the time..."

Alis laughed again, and Jon wished he could just tell her the truth.

You can, his bear said, and Jon sighed.

Not here, I can't. She's not a shifter, and I can't exactly change into a bear to prove myself in the middle of a diner.

The bear looked around a little wistfully. *But then we could eat everything.*

Yes, Jon said dryly, *while the rest of the patrons ran away screaming. It's not a good idea.*

His bear sighed even more melodramatically than Jon himself had, and fell silent as Jon found his way back to the thread of the conversation. "Anyway, then once we got older and got involved in running the tavern, there was never any time to learn. And now I'm getting old enough to feel creaky and it seems like a less-good idea. Even the armored sword fights seem like too much work now."

"Oh yes. You must be ancient. All of what, thirty-two?"

Jon did his best to look offended. "I'll have you know I'm only thirty. For another few weeks, anyway."

Alis put her hand over her heart and bowed slightly. "Please forgive me, my lord. Your wisdom and kindness hath confused mine eye, mistaking thy good heart for experienced years."

"And here I thought being nice kept you young."

"Oh, hush, I was trying! I'm not good at improv!"

Jon grinned. "I think you're just fine at it. Look, can I give you a lift back to the fairgrounds? Since we're heading the same direction anyway?"

"Aw, I'd love to, but—" Alis glanced toward the parking lot. "I've got all my costuming stuff with me, so I need to drive myself back. But I'll see you at the lists?"

"Yes, although it's a good thing you're not fighting," Jon said, looking over the impressive number of plates she'd cleared. "You'll be in a food coma before noon."

"Aaah, you'd be surprised." Alis winked at him and went to pay her bill. Over Jon's objections, she also paid his, and shrugged it off. "You can buy me a beer and a turkey leg at the faire."

"It's a date," he said hopefully, and to his relief, Alis responded with a blinding smile.

"It *is* a date."

CHAPTER 8

ALIS WAS BEAMING when she got back in the RV. Jasmine crawled into the driver's seat with a relieved, "*Whew*. I was afraid I'd blown it for you. Sorry, I totally panicked and ran."

"It's okay, we got it figured out. And I have a date!"

"Oooh, sister! Do I need to clear out of the RV tonight?"

"Oh, God, I don't think so. We're going for turkey legs and beer, not roses and romance. But it's still nice."

Jazz beamed back at her in the rear-view mirror. "Yeah, it is. He seemed nice, for the five seconds I was freaking out at him. All right, get dressed. You took so long with breakfast you're barely going to make it in time."

Alis scrambled into her court gown and fixed her hair, jewelry and makeup before taking a selfie so Jazz would have a reference photo for when she needed to dress up, later. Then she blew her sister a kiss as

Jasmine paused at the front gates to drop her off, and Alis hopped out of the RV to join the faire.

A sing-song of *I have a date!* ran through Alis's head all morning. It was silly, but the tune kept running through her mind anyway. *I have a daaa-aaate!* It kept her smiling as she greeted everyone in the Red Court, and as they played out their story, with the King and Queen encouraging the men and women of their court waiting to find romance as true as their own. Alis and a few others, men and women alike, went to the lists together, chattering in Faire-style speech and pausing to admire children, shops, and potential suitors along the way.

None of them held a candle to Jon Torben, Alis decided cheerfully. Of course, they weren't meant to: mostly the court members flirted with 'commoners,' the faire attendees, to make them feel like they were part of the experience. It was fun, but Alis couldn't wait to see Jon again, and was glad they were early enough to get good viewing spots for the second day of unarmored fighting.

Jon saw her as he was coming into the battle ring, and struck his fist against his heart in a salute. Alis waved her handkerchief and got a ribald comment from the woman at her side, whom she elbows in return. "I saw him first."

"He got his ass handed to him yesterday," one of the young men of the court said. He was tall and slim and his in-character name was Ronan. "It's a very fine ass, but I bet he lands on it again today."

"I think he'll cover himself in glory," Alis said with confidence.

"Ooooh. Lady Alessandra has chosen herself a champion!" Ronan let go an ear-piercing whistle and yelled, "Fight well, Armsman! Your lady awaits!"

Jon flashed a brilliant grin in their direction and took a bow that made the people around Alis go *oooOOOoooh* and tease her as the fights got underway. When Jon's turn came, he *did* fight well, showing off the skill he'd displayed yesterday until Alis had distracted him. But yesterday he'd been playing to the crowd, too, and today he was more focused, clearly determined to win. After a while Ronan, next to Alis, muttered a reluctant, "God damn," and she grinned at him.

"I should have bet you on it."

"Good thing you didn't, my lady, or I'd have lost that wager." He hooted and applauded, though, when Jon was declared the victor, and offered Alis a polite arm as the unarmored fights came to an end.

"My thanks, good sir." She let Ronan lead her up to the celebration dais, where eventually the winners of the entire tourney would be honored. For now, the courtiers took advantage of its extra height to make a performance of offering their favors to their chosen knights, squires, and fighters. To Alis's delight, Ronan offered a rainbow favor to a good-looking bearded knight with dark hair and eyes, and the man blushed with pleasure. Alis murmured, "I see you've a champion yourself, good sir," and Ronan winked at her.

Jon, coming up next, *hmph*ed good-naturedly at

Ronan. "Is that my competition? He's pretty, but I could break him in half."

"There is no need, Armsman. I hold space in my heart for only one man." Alis bent to tie her favor—red to match her gown—around his upper arm, and for a moment found herself tempted to just fall forward into his arms.

The problem with that was it would cause a whole scene. A literal scene, with people responding to the image of a maiden swooning into a guardsman's arms. It could take a solid hour to extract herself from the performance, and she was supposed to be in the fighting ring herself in forty-five minutes. As it was, she barely had time to praise and admire Jon properly before she had to go change into her armor and switch Jasmine into the role of Lady Alessandra.

For the first time she could ever remember, Alis wished she *wasn't* fighting as the Black Knight. Swooning into Jon's arms sounded like more fun. Even if it meant having to improvise her way through the scene it would cause, and it was very clear after that morning's near-disaster at the diner that improvisation really *wasn't* Alis's strong suit.

"Alis?" Jon spoke her name softly, drawing her all the way into the moment instead of lingering at its edges with regret. "Are you all right?"

He sounded so concerned, as if there was nothing more important in all the world than making certain she *was* okay. His dark eyes were locked on her, gentle, caring, and deep enough to drown in. Alis wanted to kiss him as much as she wanted to fall into his arms, but *that* would cause a scene, too. Frustration or anger must have shown in her face, because Jon drew back a little, obviously worried he'd overstepped.

She caught his arm, or rather, the favor on his arm, holding him tight. "I just wish I could stay here with you forever."

"We might be able to arrange that." Without further warning, Jon swept her into his arms. Alis shrieked with surprise. The entire gathered audience burst into spontaneous applause and cheers as Jon cradled her close, the way he held her so effortless that Alis forgot how to breathe.

She remembered again a heartbeat later as a ranking member of the Silver Court who had joined them at the lists—a blond, elfin man who was probably wearing a wig, but wore it well—shouted, "Unhand that maiden, you blaggard!"

Alis, not quite in character, yelled, "The maiden doesn't wish to be unhanded!"

Laughter rose, but in storytelling terms, she definitely *wasn't* supposed to be swept off by a low-ranking armsman. Jon, from right up close, murmured, "Crap. Should I fight him for your honor or something? Sorry, I got carried away!"

"Lady, I fear your honor has been compromised!" Lord Argent shouted. "That, and perhaps your good sense! Peasant! Release the lady and I shall teach you a lesson about putting your hands on your betters!"

An incredibly stubborn expression came over Jon's face, and Alis thought, *Oh no.*

Stubbornness fixing his jaw in place, Jon turned slowly toward Lord Argent with Alis still in his arms.

Argent had a foxy sort of appeal to him, sharp features, a longish nose, a slim but strong build that his Renaissance faire garb, in silver and white, made the most of. Alis hadn't interacted with him before in their shared Court, but caught a glimpse of an emblem on his shoulder, and groaned very quietly. "I know him," she breathed against Jon's shoulder.

Well, *she* didn't know him, but the Black Knight had crossed swords with him more than once. "He's brilliant with a sword," she said, still under her breath. "Left-handed, but fights with his right."

"Shit," Jon murmured. "Inigo Montoya?"

"If he's losing, yeah."

"How do people beat him?"

"With a stick, while he sleeps."

Jon's gaze jerked to hers and he laughed, then put her on the ground and bowed gallantly to Argent. "The lady has a small fear of heights, my lord. She only asked to be helped down from the dais. I meant no insult, and am sure she can defend her honor without my meagre assistance, as her tongue and wit are as sharp and magnificent as her beauty."

Alis swore Argent's expression soured for a moment before he bowed gallantly and swept a hand over his heart as he met Alis's eyes. "Then forgive me, lady fair, for not assuming you had asked for help, but instead assumed that this scoundrel had taken liberties. Perhaps you will do me the honor of considering me for a favor in the armored fights later this afternoon, as

I know this miscreant lacks the skill, time, and talent for such endeavors."

"I will miscreant your ass," Jon said through a smile, so quietly that Alis was obviously the only person who could hear him.

She fought off the impulse to shoot him a huge grin, and instead managed a polite smile toward Argent. "My favor shall go to the best in the ring, my lord, as always."

Which meant Lord Edward absolutely had to kick Argent's skinny white butt.

CHAPTER 9

Jon had lost his mate.

He was reasonably confident it wasn't a permanent sort of thing, but they'd been at the lists facing off with that tooth-grindingly-annoying Lord Argent, and then Alis had disappeared. To be fair, Jon wouldn't have wanted to hang around with Argent giving him smarmy smiles, either, but he'd thought Alis wouldn't just abandon him. He'd asked the guy who'd been with her—the man introduced himself as Ronan—but he shrugged away any knowledge of where Alis had gone.

We'll see our mate again, his bear promised him. *If we go to the next fights, our mate will be there.*

"I know, but..." Jon sighed and lumbered through the fairgrounds feeling particularly tragic about it all. *I don't like that Argent guy and I wish she'd stuck near me, that's all.*

He didn't know much about 'Lord Argent,' except that the man, like the Black Knight, traveled around to different Renaissance Faires to fight and court and whatever else he did. He wasn't in business the way Jon and Laurie were. Jon vaguely thought Faires *were* his business: that he was a professional actor who jobbed his way around the country by playing elfin lords at the faires. Whatever his deal was, Jon didn't like him. He smelled bad. Arrogant. Stuck-up. Something. Jon wasn't actually sure those things had scent, but he *felt* like they did, just now.

We could swat him, his bear said hopefully. *Hard enough that he'd fly into a mountain and be eaten by birds!*

I'll keep it on the list of possibilities. Jon was oddly heartened by his bear's…well, he wasn't sure if 'helpfulness' was really the right word, but he'd go with it.

The tavern was packed when he finally arrived. Bar swains—the male equivalent of the wenches, at least according to what Jon had read about Shakespearian-era words—were moving double-time, lifting trays of beer above everybody's heads while the wenches served from behind the bar. After hours, the girls got out from behind the bar, but during the day, male servers worked the floor because they were less likely to get groped. The tavern had been run that way as long as Jon could remember, probably because his mother had been in charge of it back in the day.

Laurie, who was obviously moving more easily today but still couldn't take his knee brace off, waved vigorously after delivering a tray to a group of sunburned fairgoers. "Where've you been, man? I'm working my ass off here!"

"Yeah, that's how my summers usually go, Laur. I'm sweating like a pig—"

*A **bear**.*

Bears don't sweat! "—while you're out gallivanting with the girls. Kinda sucks, doesn't it?"

Wow, he was in a mood. Laurie took half a step back, surprised and injured, but the thing was, Jon wasn't *wrong*. He just didn't usually complain directly to his brother about it.

For a guilty moment, he remembered their cousin Ashley's frustration with both of them, and how she'd had to be equally direct with Jon to get him to pull his weight. Getting a wake-up call wasn't all that comfortable. Before Laurie could say anything, Jon added, "I've got to get back to the lists to watch the armored fights, but I can help with the crush for about half an hour. It looks like it's been a great day."

"Yeah," Laurie said, and after a few seconds, shook off whatever he was feeling. "Yeah, it's been really busy all day. I've had to bounce a few dudes for bad behavior, but mostly people are loving it. Especially when the minstrels are here. They're on break for a while, though. I thought Peter was going to pass out from sun stroke. I swear he's got the sense God gave a goose."

"I seem to remember Mom saying the same thing about you." Jon grabbed one of the tavern's bear-logo tunics to pull over his blousy shirt, marking himself as one of the employees, and spent closer to an hour serving the noisy, cheerful crowd. It finally began to loosen up a little as the wind caught scents from the barbecue place down the way, and Jon cornered Laurie again before he headed out. "Do you know anything about Lord Argent?"

"I know I can't beat him," Laurie said. "I've gone up against him at two fairs and gotten my ass kicked both times. Oh, is that why you were all bitchy? Did he give you a smackdown?"

"No, he was putting moves on Alis."

Laurie's eyes widened and his voice dropped. "On your mate? The girl mate, at least?"

Jon had *almost* let himself forget about the complications of finding his mate, and groaned, but nodded. "Yeah, the girl mate. I still haven't met Lord Edward."

Laurie's eyes got bigger. "Oh, shit, that's why you need to go to the lists. Dude, go! Go go go! Bring him back if you can, I gotta meet this guy! Oh, and also totally kick Argent's butt, the guy's kind of a dick."

"I don't fight in the armored division," Jon pointed out, then squinted at his brother. "Neither do you. How'd you end up fighting him?"

"He only dropped the unarmored fights last year. Before that he liked to do all three of the tourney fights, but you know how beat up you get doing any one of them. I guess he decided two was enough. Didn't want to risk breaking that pointy nose of his again."

Jon laughed. "Again?"

"I ain't sayin' nothin'," Laurie said with aplomb. "Except maybe a couple years ago I decided if I wasn't gonna win, I'd at least leave an impression."

"Bro!"

"Dude." Laurie grinned at him. "Go meet your man."

"I was gonna go meet Alis again," Jon said weakly, but went. Part of him *was* eager to actually meet the Black Knight. Aside from that glimpse into the guy's eyes that told him everything, he knew nothing about the man. Nobody did. But there had to be something about him that meant it would work out, because fate knew what it was doing.

Doesn't it? he asked worriedly.

His bear made a content sound. *Always.*

"Okay. Then it'll be fine." He hoped.

THE FIGHTING GROUNDS were *busy* when he finally got there. Partly it was just that he'd left it too late, but also, from the chatter, a lot of people had heard about Jon's little clash with Argent, earlier. They'd shown up to watch Argent take on the Black Knight in their first round together. Nobody cared that it was basically an exhibition fight: both of them were guaranteed places in the semi-finals, which wouldn't take place for days yet. But it would be a good exhibition, meant to draw crowds, and that was the point.

Jon quashed the impulse to push his way through to the fences so he was right on the front line. For one thing, he was over six feet tall and could see over the heads of at least seventy percent of the people there. For another, it struck him that he almost never stopped to take a minute to really *look* at the faire going on around him. He hadn't for years, not since he and Laurie had taken over running the tavern. He'd steal glimpses that would stay with him a little while, but he didn't really get to be in the middle of it as a partici-pant, just reveling in what was going on round him.

And there was so *much* going on. Most attendees just came to the faire in regular everyday clothing. But an awful lot of people dressed up. Some of them, like a woman over there in a long black skirt, a puffy white peasant blouse, and a big leather belt, were pretty clearly working with what was already in their closet, but at least were capturing a little bit of the vibe. Others were in things more fantastical than Jon could even imagine wearing, like a very tall dude in a green horned faun costume that Jon vaguely recognized from a movie. For all he knew, it could've been the guy *from* the movie, the costume was that good. It was probably hot enough to melt in, too.

There was everything in between those two extremes, too. Corsets and buccaneer boots and people who were centuries out of date—he saw at least one couple who were very definitely in Regency clothes, inspired by that tv show everybody had been watching lately, probably—and the occasional science fiction renegade who just wanted a chance to dress up. Adults didn't get to do that enough, Jon thought a little wryly. He'd been doing it so regularly his whole adult life that he forgot other people kind of didn't get much chance.

A sudden cheer caught him off guard and he automatically made a noise along with everybody else, turning to see what was going on. The armored division were making their appearance: a herald called out names, but everybody around Jon was already chanting Edward's name, although it became a mishmash as Argent also arrived, waving to his fans. Jon couldn't, from this distance, catch Edward's eye again, but his bear gave a happy sigh. *Our mate.*

"But—!" Jon skimmed the lists, searching for and finally finding Lady Alessandra, wearing pale green with a jewel in her hair, just as she had been earlier. She was laughing and waving to the knights with a fluttering handkerchief just like the one she'd tied around his arm earlier…

…and there was no spark at all.

Of course not, his bear said. *That's not our mate.* **That's our mate.** It made a picture of Edward's helm in his head.

Jon gestured wildly toward the gathering of courtly folk who were watching the fights begin. *But Alis is right there!*

Lord Edward is our mate, his bear replied placidly.

But why does it keep switching back and forth? Jon asked desperately. *Doesn't it have to be both—*

A shock slammed through him so hard that he staggered. Somebody grabbed at him, helping him stay upright, and then a number of people were basically passing him along, getting him out of the crowd and out of the heat. He vaguely heard someone call for a medic, and a minute later found himself sitting in a tent with a fan blowing directly on him while a medic in a healing tunic pressed a glass of Gatorade into his hand. "A healing potion," the medic said with a brief smile. "You need electrolytes."

"Yeah, I…thanks." Jon took a sip, found it delicious, and drank the whole thing, because if a power drink tasted good it meant he needed it. The medic handed him another one, and he sipped at that one, staring blankly at the tent wall.

He hadn't considered the possibility that he would have to *choose* between his mates. That was the only reason he could think that he kept running hot and cold on Alis. Sometimes she was the perfect woman for him, and other times…other times, apparently Lord Edward was his perfect mate. Maybe if he could get them side by side—

"But they *were*," he whispered, almost wailed, to himself. He'd watched Alis tie the favor around Edward's arm, and if that wasn't them being side by side, Jon didn't know what was. And his bear said Edward was his mate, in that case.

But Alis was fabulous. With those sharp strong features she'd called hatchet-like, but which made up the most gorgeous face he'd ever seen. With her quick wit, and her soft mouth, and her absolutely impossible appetite…how could any *guy* hope to compete? Except his heart leaped with certainty every time he saw Edward, and only sometimes when he saw Alis.

Jon put his face in his hands. "I don't know how to do this. I don't even know how to find Edward to talk to him. He disappears into the crowd when the fights are over."

He hadn't meant anybody to overhear, but the medic chuckled. "Crushing on the Black Knight? Join the line. Everybody says he comes to the faires as a commoner and that's why nobody's ever figured out who he is. He's just a face in the crowd until it's time to put that armor on."

Jon nodded into his hands. "That's what I've heard, yeah. There must be some people who are in on it, because he'd need somewhere to change clothes, but…"

"You know it's a fantasy, right?" the medic asked gently. Jon blinked up at him, and the man, in his fifties and kind-looking, smiled. "The Black Knight is a fantasy. Whoever is inside that armor gets tired and grumpy and hungry just like everyone else. The reason their identity has been kept secret this long is that people want the fantasy and they're afraid if they find out the truth, they'll be disappointed. Collectively, fair-goers have decided they'd rather have the secret than the reality."

Alis is real. Jon wasn't certain if he was talking to his bear or himself, but he nodded slowly. Even if his certainty about her switched on and off…well, maybe fated mates weren't as absolutely certain as everybody said they were. After all, nobody really liked to admit doubts about their partners, especially when the romance was fresh and new and exciting. Maybe it just wasn't quite as perfect as everyone pretended.

That would make a lot more sense than chasing a fantasy.

"Thank you," he said after a long minute. "For the Gatorade and the wisdom."

The medic chuckled. "My pleasure, young man. Now remember to stay hydrated, all right? And not just water. You do need those electrolytes."

"I'll do my best," Jon promised, and went in search of his fated mate.

CHAPTER 10

ALIS AND LORD Argent sat across the lists from each other, glaring across the distance like they could fight their battles with their minds as well as their bodies. Their upcoming clash wouldn't affect their rankings: they were both already slotted in the semi-finals that week, and would both be taking part in the afternoon of jousting that was the last, showy spectacle for the faire.

Everybody else was in it for the competition. Alis kept making herself take her eyes off Argent so she could pay attention to the people who might become her opponents. She liked to know what fighting styles she was facing before they met in the ring, and it had helped her win for years.

But Argent was such a smug bastard, she just wanted to punch him in the teeth with a gauntleted fist. How *dare* he pretend he was coming to her rescue by accusing Jon of dishonorable behavior! How dare he position himself as the hero, when she was already making her preferences *quite clear*, thank you! And how dare he be so cavalier about defeating the Black Knight, when he'd failed to do so for five years running! Alis yanked her attention away from Argent again, scowling through her helm's slender eye slits at the up-and-coming opponents.

Several of them were very good, and had put time and effort into their armor. Alis was preposterously grateful for the lightweight metal compounds available in the modern world. She might be a tall, strong woman, but the forty pounds of steel that knights of old wore would have dragged her down faster than she cared to think about. These days, the same kind of protection could be had for a lot less weight. One of the signs of somebody serious about the art of fighting was the quality of their armor.

Of course, it was also a terrible money pit, so there were a lot of people who were very serious about the tourneys who never went beyond the non-armored sword fights that Jon was participating in. Alis was lucky to have enough disposable income to spend on her dreams, although the flip side of that was she hadn't been on a vacation that wasn't to a ren faire since her whole family had gone to Disneyland for her and Jasmine's sixteenth birthday.

Jazz was over there waving a handkerchief and fluttering like a ditzy fair lady far better than Alis ever did. It was almost too bad her twin only wanted to spend a few hours a day, at most, doing faire activities. She was a much better actress than Alis herself was, and it was fun to watch her flirt coyly and swoon over the knights.

She probably would have a better way to handle Argent than 'break his teeth,' but Alis had needed to do such a quick change into the Black Knight's armor that she hadn't been able to ask for some sisterly advice. Maybe after the fight, which was coming up fast now. Alis rose, stretching, and a cheer went up for just that. A few minutes later, she and Argent were in the ring, both of them putting on a performance for the cat-calling crowd. Once in a while she would break away from the fight to play to the audience, cupping a hand at her ear to suggest she couldn't hear them, or lifting her hands up, up, up again to encourage the cries. Argent did the same, although Alis didn't think she imagined that his supporters weren't as loud.

The second time she played to the crowd, Argent rushed her, despite the fact she'd left him gasping for air. She took a hell of a hit across her right ribcage, but didn't fall to the ground, which was clearly his hope. Then the battle was engaged again, swords slamming together, metal ringing, the ferocity of genuine dislike pushing the fight to new heights. Alis pulled a move she'd done with him before, sliding under his blade to twist back toward him with hers, and had just enough time to think: *that was a mistake,* before it all came crashing down.

It was something in his palm, a flash of incredibly bright white light that sliced through her visor and blinded her. She knew his moves well enough to block the first attack after that even with green and white brilliance wreaking havoc with her vision, but the second attack swept low, which Argent never did with opponents shorter than he. Alis's feet went out from under her, and though she rolled, she couldn't move fast enough: all at once, his blade was at her throat.

The exhibition fight was over.

She had lost.

"I CAN'T EVEN COMPLAIN," Alis growled to Jasmine later, as they pulled her armor off. "I can't keep my damn voice at a low enough pitch long enough to pass for male."

"You could tell the truth and shame the devil," Jasmine suggested. She was almost as angry as Alis. Maybe more so, having watched her twin go down in an ignominious heap and having been helpless to do anything about it, only to have it made worse by finding out Argent had cheated.

Alis groaned. "God, no, not now, not after a loss. If I'm going to do a dramatic reveal it's got to be on a massive win. Otherwise I'll always be the girl who lost to Lord Argent of Snottypantsshire."

Jasmine obviously couldn't help the laugh. "I'm going to start calling him that in public. I bet it'll catch on. But you could say you saw it from the stands," she said more seriously. "His back was to me right then, but you could say you say you saw him doing that earlier in the bout. He has to have tried more than once to catch you. That visor's really well designed to protect your eyes from flares."

"He probably did try, but what if he didn't?" Alis sighed. "I'm just going to have to be wary in the competition round and really humiliate him."

"That's my sweet, charming sister." Jasmine hugged Alis once they'd gotten all her armor off, then tilted her head back toward the fair. "Go find your sword boy and work out some of that frustration."

"Jasmine," Alis said with a gasp of mock shock. "Whatever are you suggesting?"

"Probably seeing who can drink who under the table," Jasmine said, and Alis laughed.

"He owns a brewery. I don't think I stand a chance. But, um, you know, I'll text if I'm not coming home tonight?"

"Yeah, you will, because you don't want your best sister to worry." Jasmine sighed heavily. "You're sure you're all right? He got a couple nasty hits in."

"I'll walk it off," Alis promised. "No, really, I'm okay. Thanks for worrying, though."

"As always. I'm going back to the RV to work after this, unless you need me around?"

"I'm good. Go do your genius stuff. I love you, Jazz."

"I love you too, you big weirdo." Jasmine began packing up her computer from their little changing-booth-tent as Alis made her way back to the faire proper, still fuming quietly over Argent's cheating. She should go to the Red Court to wrap up the evening performances, but if she had to see his face again right now, she was afraid she actually would punch that pointy nose. Somebody *had* broken it, she recalled with delight. A couple of years earlier at a faire out East. After he'd beaten some young man in the unarmored division, the other guy had gotten one last hit in on Argent's helm, cracking his nose with the nose piece.

That made her feel quite a lot better, even though it probably shouldn't. And Lady Alessandra didn't know Argent had cheated, so she had to stop sulking and be charming and delightful and fluttery about how the Crimson Knight had defeated the Black in the exhibition round.

Well, maybe that was pushing it a little too far. Jasmine, as Alessandra, had given the Black Knight her favor anyway, so Alis didn't need to *flutter* about Argent. She rejoined the Red Court at their magnificent tent, accepted a cold drink from somebody, and sat down for a moment to watch and listen.

The tent was huge, partitioned into a 'backstage' changing area and a main event space. The king and queen had thrones that could be rolled out of the tent for public scenes and proclamations, and there were other chairs scattered around the interior for the members of the court. Fans were set up in every corner so that the air moved, which helped a little with the heat. It was all lush and red and gold, keeping in theme with the court's title.

The Red Queen, a luminously gorgeous woman whose delicate crown nestled into cornrowed braids, was carrying one of those USB-powered hand fans and currently in conversation with a small child who was arguing that it was modern technology, while the queen explained that she believed it to be astonishing magic created by the court sorcerer. Her husband, the Red King—and Alis thought they might actually be married—was a tall lean man whose black eyes sparkled as he listened to his queen explain the 'magic' of her fan. Their 'daughter,' Princess Cecilia, was a local woman whose real-life sister made perfume that everybody in the court tried to avoid wearing, because it was genuinely awful but nobody had the heart to tell her. The whole royal family were spectacularly dressed in the style of Henry the Eighth, showing off the same reds and golds that Alis wore.

In fact, the entire court was in red, so they could be easily identified as actors and performers at the faire, rather than 'commoners.' Alis looked better in green, and had badly wanted to buck the trend, but the whole point was to blend in. Drawing attention to herself could jeopardize her double life as the Black Knight, and it would be a shame to do that at this late stage.

The other court members ranged from kids who clearly belonged with some of the adults, to an elderly couple who had been participating in Renaissance's faire since it started more than thirty years ago. The man, Stuart, was currently playing the role of court sorcerer, and turned out to have a fantastic repertoire of magic tricks that ended up enthralling the argumentative child. Alis slid deeper in her chair, drinking what turned out to be a root beer, and watching with a smile.

Eloise, the woman of the pair, came to sit down by her. "This is your first Faire, isn't it?"

"My first Renaissance faire," Alis agreed, then

laughed. "I mean, my first one *in* Renaissance. I go to quite a few back East."

"Aaah. Stew and I just do this one." She smiled fondly at her husband as he pulled a coin out of the child's ear, then settled back with a sigh. "It's a shame this will be the last, though, after so long."

Alis straightened, the root beer turning to a cold hard lump as it slid down her throat. "The last? What? I hadn't heard that!"

"Oh. Oh dear. Well. Stuart retired from the bank, you know, but he's still got contacts there and someone let slip that the fairgrounds were being sold. It's all supposed to be very hush-hush. I'm sure you won't say a word." Eloise gave her a pointed look, determination glittering in her pale blue eyes.

A thread of humor twisted itself around the knot that had formed in Alis's belly. "Of course not," she said obligingly. "I'm only an outsider with no business getting involved in Renaissance's affairs."

"Precisely. I'd never say anything to the locals. I wouldn't want to be seen as a gossip."

Alis thought she might love this old woman. "Obviously not. Nothing wrong with sharing a bit of news with somebody who's got no oar in the race, though. Who did you say was buying the fairgrounds, again? And what on earth for? They can't possibly need to put up a parking lot."

"I have the impression it's primarily to put the faire out of business," Eloise said crisply. "You know how sometimes people try to trademark and copyright common phrases? Oh, like that cable television company—" She broke off, eyeing Alis. "You do know what cable TV is, don't you, young lady? You are aware that streaming services aren't the only way people watch television?"

Alis laughed. "Yes, but I'm not sure I blame you for asking."

Eloise gave a brief satisfied nod. "So when that one company couldn't trademark 'sci-fi' because it's a common phrase for science fiction, so they changed their name to that silly spelling. And—oh, dear. I'm a very old geek, my dear, and I'm afraid my references might not make any sense to you."

Alis leaned toward her, smiling. "If you tell me you were part of the original letter-writing campaign that got Star Trek saved, I'm going to worship you."

The old woman's eyes lit up. "Not quite that old, but maybe you do have some frame of reference. Do you go to comics conventions?"

"I know about the one in San Diego...?" That was about all Alis knew about comics, but it seemed to satisfy Eloise.

"There's a corporation that does international comics conventions a little like San Diego's," she said. "They've got a trademarked name and all. And there's a movement toward trying to incorporate Renaissance faires under the same kind of trademark. But—"

The pieces suddenly fell into place. "But they want to use the phrase 'Renaissance Faire' in their trademark. But this town is *called* Renaissance, so anybody who wants to use that is going to have to shut this faire down completely, because nobody can stop Renaissance, Colorado from using…well, like, 'Renaissance's Faire,' at the very least, and that'll confuse the corporate issue," Alis guessed.

"Very good."

"But…" Alis gazed at the old woman for a moment. "This can't be news, right? People must know somebody's trying to make a big business out of ren fairs?"

"Oh, yes." Eloise went back to watching her husband, as if they were discussing nothing of any particular importance. "And there's a lot of resistance to that, of course. But the paperwork to buy the fairgrounds here was just filed on Friday afternoon, very quietly. Stew and I think it's a targeted attack on Renaissance's faire itself and they're trying to push it through quickly, so no one has time to mount a resistance."

"Who?" Alis dropped her voice to a whisper, as if they were back-room scheming.

Eloise sighed. "I wish I knew, darling, but even if it wasn't hidden behind some labyrinth of corporate shells, Stew's friends at the bank couldn't give him a name. They only mentioned the sale in passing." Her eyes glittered again, and Alis was certain it hadn't been an accidental mention. Somebody in the bank at Renaissance didn't want the faire to collapse.

She couldn't imagine *anybody* in town wanted it to collapse. Alis was only here for the first two weekends, but the faire ran for eight weeks every summer and brought in a huge amount of tourism. She guessed there was probably skiing on the mountain in the winter, but even just driving through town on her way to the fairgrounds, it was clear that Renaissance, Colorado leaned into its name and its faire as a major part of its marketing.

"Well. This has been a very interesting conversation." She slid a little smile toward Eloise. "I think I'll go talk to some strangers about something else entirely."

"Oh, what a good idea, my dear. But may I make a suggestion? Change your clothes, so when you talk about something else, it won't be associated with the Red Court."

"Oh, you *are* clever," Alis said with a grin, and the old woman sat back with an expression that managed to be both beatifically innocent and incredibly smug. Alis got up and went into the changing area, where she *did* have commoner clothes, just in case of emergency. She came out a few minutes later in denim shorts, a green tank top, and sandals, all of which felt much more comfortable in the warm tent than her gown had. She caught Eloise's eye, and the old woman pointed to her own hair. Alis put her hand up, found that she was still wearing the Red Court haircomb from earlier, and took it out, sending her mess of curls down over her shoulders.

Eloise gave her a thumbs up and Alis, grinning, went out to spread rumors at the faire.

CHAPTER 11

"Have you heard anything about the fairgrounds being sold?" Peter, the fiddler who looked like an imp and played like an angel, stomped into the tavern as the evening drew to a close. The patrons were mostly gone; it was Sunday evening and the faire closed early to make getting up on Monday morning a little easier. For the next few days, the big event stuff like the sword fights and human chess games would be on hold, until attendance picked up again on Friday afternoon.

Jon, in the midst of wiping tables down, straightened and stared at Peter incredulously. "No. What? Are you serious?"

"It's all over the faire. Can I get a pint of Thunder Blunder, Laurie?"

"Yes," Jon said automatically, then, thinking about it, added, "but this one's not on the house, Pete."

The fiddler looked injured. Laurie, behind the counter, hissed, "Dude!"

"Believe it or not, we are trying to run a business

here, and you get drinks during the sessions *and* after hours free," Jon said. "You can afford to pay for one drink."

"Sure and a single drink will never quench me thirst," Peter said in a passable Irish accent completely unlike his own Californian one.

Jon snorted. "Then buy two. Who told you the fairgrounds were being sold? Laurie, have you heard anything about this?"

His brother made a face. "A couple of the patrons mentioned it about an hour ago, but I told them it would never happen, that it was just a dumb rumor. There isn't anything to it, is there?"

"There can't be," Jon said a bit stupidly. "Why would somebody even want the fairgrounds? What would they do with them?"

"Parking for the ski lodges up the mountain?" Laurie asked dubiously. "You know our traffic laws get their panties in a bunch."

The three of them, all Renaissance natives, grinned a bit at each other. Renaissance had been settled over a century ago by shifters, and their back-to-nature wilderness vibe had brought a huge influx of hippies into the town in the sixties and seventies. One of the many things the two communities could agree on was prioritizing people over vehicles. When ski resorts had started to move in shortly after the hippies arrived, the town council had provided a united front against paving Renaissance with parking lots for the resorts' convenience. Decades later it was still a point of contention.

"Yeah, but..." Jon ended up shaking his head. "Tons of people stay at the lodges during the faire, so they get all kinds of summer business that they wouldn't if this was a parking lot. That doesn't mean it can't be them, but...was somebody else interested in taking it over? Running the faire, I mean?"

Laurie made a face. "Then they'd run for the committee. I guess probably most places don't have an elected town committee for their faires, but most places aren't Renaissance."

"Believe me, it was the only way to make it work," Peter muttered. He'd been on the committee for at least twenty years. Jon was pretty sure he'd actually helped set it up. In fact, he launched into a lecture that Jon and Laurie both already knew pretty well, having heard it from their parents many times. "We couldn't rely just on volunteers and handing it over to a new batch of fair-runners every year, and there are so many businesses in Renaissance that rely on the faire—"

"—that incorporating it as a town-run function was the only thing that made sense," the two younger Torben brothers chorused along with him.

Peter's jaw snapped shut and he eyed both of them. Laurie, grinning, brought him the pale ale he'd asked for, and, despite Jon's admonishment, said, "On the house. But wouldn't the committee be the first people to hear about if somebody was trying to buy the fairgrounds?"

"Yes, which is why I don't like it!" Peter drank the beer like he was proving a point, and sat down hard on one of the picnic benches. "It's probably just a rumor," he said grumpily.

"What if I'd heard it from a reliable source?" Alis's voice floated softly over the little gathering. Jon's heart leaped and he turned toward her, hoping that his bear would once more see her as their mate.

It did, with a satisfied grunt of sound that sent a wave of relief through Jon. But then he realized what she'd said, and waved her in. "What are you talking about?"

She had abandoned her courtly wear and looked like a commoner, dressed in jeans shorts and a v-neck green t-shirt that dropped far enough down to be distracting. Jon told himself firmly that her eyes were *up there*, and kept his gaze above her collarbones.

Which was less helpful than it might have been, honestly. For one, she had great collarbones that made pleasing lines to emphasize her wide shoulders, and for another, her hair was down and all full of thick bouncing curls that begged to have his fingers sunk into them. And if he looked higher, then he had that lovely full mouth and those magnificent bladed features to gaze at, and those deep green eyes to fall into.

Yeah, there was nowhere safe to rest his gaze, and that was the most wonderful thing he'd ever had to deal with. To his delight, she came straight over to his side and slid her arm around his waist like it was natural and comfortable. His bear gave a huge, contented sigh as Alis tilted her chin up so she could see him as she spoke. "Do you know Eloise and Stuart Presington?"

Jon said, "Yeah, of course," and his idiot brother said, "They've been coming to the faire for hundreds of years," which made Peter give him a dirty look.

"They *have* been coming since it began, but I never could get them to join the committee. Still, they know everything there is to know about it." The older man's face tightened. "Ah, hell. Are they the source of this rumor?"

"I couldn't say," Alis said primly, "but yeah. Eloise mentioned all casually that some contact Stuart still has at the bank—?" She made it a question that the men around her nodded in response to.

"Stuart was the bank manager for decades until he retired, what, five years ago now? And Eloise taught elementary school. Honestly, I think those two know every single secret Renaissance has ever had," Jon said. "But the reason they know them is they don't ever *tell* anybody."

Alis sighed. "I got the impression it was an outside offer, so maybe their secret-keeping only extends to locals. But also, she's not the one who told you guys, either, is she. She was obviously, like really obviously, making sure that if the leak circled back to anybody it would be me, another outsider. But the paperwork got filed late Friday afternoon."

"A fact which you, an outsider, would know how?" Peter asked.

Jon's bear grumbled, but he quashed it. *He's not chal-lenging her,* he promised the beast within. *He's just trying to make sure there's some kind of story that would keep the Presingtons out of it, which...*

He needn't have worried. Alis, blandly, said, "My sister is *really* good with computers," which made Peter first blink, then chuckle.

"Got a white hat in the family?"

"Honestly, I don't think she's ever hacked a thing in her life, but if you need some kind of excuse for me to know about the sale, that's vague enough to be an answer."

"Yeah, I guess so. You're a smart cookie, aren't you?"

Alis looked pained and Jon had a moment of wondering if Peter had *ever* had a partner, or if the man's fiddle was his constant companion because he condescended to women. "Who owns the fairgrounds now?"

"The town," Peter replied promptly. "Which means a sale would have to go through the town council, which..."

"Should have been a huge local issue," Jon finished. "Is it even legal for them to sell off township land without asking for public input?"

Unexpectedly, Laurie said, "Yeah," then looked defensive as Jon gaped at him. "What? You remember a few years ago when they widened the sidewalks down First and Fourth? The town claimed eminent domain on part of my buddy's front yard and we spent like a week looking up all the laws to see if they could do that. They could, because it was for the public good, but I read a bunch of other stuff and the short version is, yeah, they can *sell* township land without any input, they just can't make a land grab on somebody's yard or whatever without justifying it. In theory even the

Mayor could just sign off on something without the town council's approval."

After a pause, Jon said, "Well, shit," and Peter, who had been looking hopeful, collapsed back into the benches.

"Why the hell would anybody buy it, though?"

"This is speculation," Alis said, "but Eloise thinks there's a conglomerate trying to trademark the name 'Renaissance Faire' and Renaissance—"

A groan rose from all three men as they followed her partial explanation through to its logical conclusion. Laurie went up to the till to ring up the patrons who were waiting to pay for their drinks, turned away a last hopeful who was making his way toward the closing gates, and returned to the table. "How are we going to fight this?"

"The first thing we have to do is find out if the land has already been sold or if they've submitted paperwork that still has to be signed," Jon said. "But either way, we raise hell."

"I just can't imagine anybody on the council agreeing to this," Pete said quietly. "Even if they didn't know the fair itself might be under threat, why would they sell the land at all? It must have been a hell of a lot of money." He rubbed a hand over his eyes. "And not just for the city."

"You think someone was bribed?" Alis asked, almost as softly. She leaned into Jon a little, encouraging him to move forward and sit down at the table with Peter. For a few seconds everybody was getting themselves arranged, with Peter turning to face the table while the rest of them sat down around it. Jon glanced toward the other corner, where the musicians usually set up for the evening, but they weren't there yet.

On one hand, it was Sunday, and that always meant an earlier night. On the other, the empty table gave Jon a terrible sensation of loss, like the whole faire was slipping through their fingers and there was nothing to be done about it.

Peter was shaking his head at Alis. "Yeah. I think so, but I also can't imagine how much money it would take. These people, they've got integrity. Oh, I know, there's no such thing as a politician that can't be bought, but..." He pressed a calloused hand against his forehead, and Jon picked up where he'd left off.

"Renaissance prides itself on being...fair, I guess. Hah. Fair." He made a gesture toward their surroundings, and felt good, at least momentarily, that Alis smiled. "Seriously, though. It's kind of a weird little town, full of hippies and—" He nearly said 'shifters' out loud, but Pete wasn't one and he hadn't explained to Alis yet. He substituted, "—artists," awkwardly, and went on. "And as a town it wants to take care of its own. Like." He moved his hands helplessly. "I remember when I was a kid there was a small homeless population here, which is really dangerous in the winters. Mom brought us to one of the town council meetings where they were discussing what to do about it."

He lifted his eyes, meeting his little brother's. "And Laurie was so bored. So was I, but he was sitting there squirming and listening and just bored out of his mind and he finally stood up on his chair and said, 'If they don't have homes, why don't we just give them some-where to live?'"

Laurie's ears turned red. "Everybody laughed at me."

"They did. And then Mom said, 'Well, why don't we?' and everybody stopped laughing," Jon reminded him. "And that summer there was basically a barn-raising. Half the town turned out to build the Haven Apartments over on the west side of town, and the homeless people were invited to move in, no strings attached. Most of them got their feet under themselves in a year or two, after that, and moved out, but there's always somebody whose life goes wrong," he said quietly. "Somebody who needs that kind of help. So people still move in and out of there when they're down on their luck, and the town does maintenance. That's the kind of town Renaissance is," he said, now turning to Alis. "We're trying, you know? We're trying to be a place that…that makes sense to kids."

To his astonishment, Alis's green eyes went glassy with tears. "That's maybe the best thing I've ever heard," she said hoarsely. "I teach elementary school, I said that, right? And kids see things in really simple terms sometimes, like you did," she said to Laurie. "What you did is incredible. You changed all those peoples' lives, just by asking why we didn't do *better*." She gave a sudden laugh, still hoarse, and stuck out her hand. "Hi. I'm Alis, by the way."

"Laurie," Laurie mumbled, shaking her hand. "I get why my brother likes you."

"Point is," Peter said a little too loudly, like they'd

embarrassed *him* somehow, "it makes it hard to see why anybody on the town council would vote to sell the fairgrounds, without at least a lot of debate and hearing about what the public thought. Even if the buyer is planning to keep the fair going, it's not good for the *town* to lose control of that land, so it doesn't make sense."

"What about blackmail?" Alis asked tentatively. "Maybe there's somebody, or somebodies, on the town council with secrets they don't want shared?"

Jon locked eyes with his brother again. They both knew half the council was made up of shifters, and although there were a lot of them in Renaissance, their existence still wasn't exactly common knowledge. Jon said, "Maybe," hesitantly, but Laurie shook his head.

"No way. They'd have to know the community had their backs. We'd figure something out."

"That would depend on what their secrets were, wouldn't it?" Alis asked, still carefully. It was clear she knew she was an outsider and didn't want to offend anybody, but that didn't mean she was wrong.

But Jon thought Laurie was right, too. If something was being held over the council's head, it probably wasn't that so many of them were shifters. The shifter community *would* do something about that. "It would have to be something really dark," he said to Laurie. "Not the usual stuff."

Both Alis and Peter gave him a funny look, at that. Peter said, "The *usual* stuff? Weed is legal in Colorado, boys. Has been for decades now."

Jon cracked a laugh despite himself. "Okay, some

other kind of usual stuff, then, I guess. Maybe the mayor likes dressing in baby clothes and being spanked."

"Oh, *God*!" Laurie threw his elbow over his eyes. "I'm never going to get that out of my head, now! Dammit, Jon!"

Jon, grinning, stood up and offered Alis his hand. "All right, well, look, it seems like we've got a fairground to save, so come on, folks, let's rally the troops."

CHAPTER 12

WHEN JON SAID 'RALLY THE TROOPS,' Alis had not expected to end up back at his family's pub surrounded by roughly nine thousand men and women who were all cut from the same basic template that Jon and Laurie were. She didn't know what she *had* expected, but definitely not that.

The pub itself was amazing. Log cabin walls, a high peaked roof, rooms that were clearly later additions, but only because they had little plaques above the doors announcing the year that room had opened. The main bar stretched down the long central room, which had a small but full-blown stage at one end and a variety of booths along a wall and more movable seating in the central area. The Colorado state flag, high on the rafters, was flanked by a host of new Pride flags and the American flag. It was a huge open welcoming space, and it appeared to be entirely filled by Jon's family, who were all talking at full, outraged volume.

Alis thought she might need to blow her cover and call Jasmine for moral support. She'd never been surrounded by so many blonds in her life. Dark blond, bright blond, honey blond, medium blond, strawberry blond, bearded blond, just *blond*. The only ones who weren't blond were clearly partners, which gave Alis a sort of semi-hysterical sense of relief. At least if this sizzling connection with Jon wasn't just a passing fancy, she wouldn't be expected to bleach her hair.

They were also all shockingly tall. Alis and Jazz were both about five ten, which usually made them visibly taller than the norm for women. In this bar full of Torbens, she was average, maybe even slightly on the short side. She said, "Is it something in the water?" out loud, not expecting anyone—even Jon, who was right beside her, talking to another Torben—to hear her.

Somebody on her other side laughed, though, and Alis turned toward a blonde woman just a couple inches taller than she, who said, "The height or the blondness?"

"Either! How did you know that's what I meant?"

"Because that's how everybody reacts when they end up in this madhouse for the first time. We've got some cousins growing up in Alaska and they're all just as tall and blond, so I don't think it's the water. I'm Ashley." Ashley offered a hand. "We're a lot, I know. At least you *are* tall. My girlfriend is five four when she tries really hard."

"I assume she savages the ankles of anyone who gives her a hard time about that." Alis shook Ashley's hand gratefully as the other woman laughed.

"Ah, yes, I see you've met her. Sorry about all this. We all got your name but you've got twenty-two to remember."

"Is that how many people are in here? I was trying to count and came up with eight hundred. You're—you're the pub manager, aren't you? Jon mentioned you. He says you kick ass."

Ashley, who was one of the honey blondes but whose skin was a much tawnier brown than most of the other Torbens', beamed. "I am, and I do, and thank you for telling me he said that. I've been doing this for about eight months and I love it but my God those boys are hard to wrangle. Well, Jon's shaped up. Laurie, though." She rolled her eyes. "Good thing he's cute."

"You're all cute," Alis said. "You all look alike. Friendly blond giants. My god, you're all golden retrievers."

Ashley laughed aloud again. "No. Not quite. But yeah, the family stamp is heavy on this crowd. The good thing about it is when people see one of us coming they know they're going to have to deal with the whole clan if things go sideways. Which it sounds like they're going to." Her dark brown eyes narrowed. "I can't believe somebody is threatening the faire. Mac, over there—" She pointed at a group of tall blonds, any one of whom could be 'Mac'—is a lawyer, though, and she's going to file an injunction at the courthouse tomorrow as soon as it opens, and Uncle Dave is in real estate, so he's already on the job there, as you can see."

That suggested Uncle Dave was the guy on the phone. Mac being a woman narrowed it down to only two of the people in the group of five, which was something. Alis blurted, "How are you all *related*?" in either shock or awe. She wasn't sure which.

"Exactly, or in general?"

"In general. I don't think I could remember exactly. There are just so many of you. How is it even possible for there to *be* that many of you?"

"Right. My dad has three brothers and two sisters. Most of them have at least two kids. Several have… more. And a bunch of us have partners and or kids now, so the numbers add up really fast. This is really only about two-thirds of us, and Jon got my mom and dad down off the mountain for this, so it's a big deal."

'Got them off the mountain' was more than Alis could deal with. She skipped that part, asking, "And Jon is your…?" instead.

"First cousin. His dad and my dad are brothers."

"Okay. That'll do me for now. Man. I have one sister and two cousins. How do you keep everybody straight?"

Ashley, without missing a beat, said, "Oh, they totally failed to keep us all straight. After all, I did mention my girlfriend," and Alis laughed. Ashley looked pleased with herself, but also shook her head. "Just keeping the cousins straight isn't that hard, but now that they're starting to have kids I'm beginning to lose track. I do now understand why the teachers just used to yell, 'Torben!' when they wanted me, though. The oldest of them had taught Dad's genera-tion so by the time it got to me and Jon and Laurie they'd already had like fifteen Torbens go through and remembering everybody's first name was a lost cause."

"Thank you," Alis said, not sure she was kidding. "I'm going to just steal that trick."

Ashley grinned. "You'll get used to us. I'll introduce you to Penny when she's in town next and you two can commiserate."

"Oh, I'm only here through next weekend."

Ashley's eyebrows rose. "Really?"

"Well, yes. I've got another faire the week after that, out in Seattle. It's the first time I've ever gotten this far west and I'm trying to make the most of it."

Ashley said, "Huh," like that was genuinely surprising news. "Well, I guess Renaissance will always be ready to welcome you back, because I think your presence is going to be the catalyst that lets us save our faire."

"Somebody would have heard about the fairgrounds being sold," Alis protested, but Ashley shook her head.

"Somebody already *should* have heard about it, is the thing. Nothing goes under the radar in a town this small. So the fact that they've gotten as far as filing paperwork without anybody knowing means they're somehow keeping a really tight lid on it, and I think it might actually have been too late if you hadn't spread the word."

Alis echoed that, "Huh," dubiously, but Ashley looked entirely serious, so Alis shrugged pleasantly. "Well, if I helped, I'm glad. It seems like a great faire and I wouldn't want anything to happen to it. Um, excuse me for a minute? I'm running later than I thought and need to call my sister to let her know I'm okay."

"No worries. Come over to the bar for a drink if you want, when you're done."

"Thank you." Alis escaped to the beer garden, which just about doubled the size of the bar: it was roofed, with heavy-duty plastic windows that could be rolled up or down, and scattered with mosquito zappers to help keep the bugs away.

It was also blessedly, blissfully *quiet* compared to the good-natured cacophony inside. Alis wandered down the steps and out into the lawn, which had picnic tables of its own to extend the pub's footprint even farther. The cheerful bear logo above the pub made her smile as she called Jasmine, who picked up with an, "Aw, I assume you're not in the middle of having great sex, if you're calling me."

"God, I hope not. That would be weird and awkward. No, I'm at the Thunder Bear Brewpub with Jon and fifteen million other people in his immediate family."

"Whoa. He took you home to meet the family already?"

"Oh, God, no, not like that. Things got a little dramatic after you left." Alis sat on one of the picnic tables, shivering a little in the night breeze and watching fireflies glimmer in and out of sight as she caught Jasmine up on the evening. She ended with a cautious, "You don't, um. You know. Ummm. Poke around in places you're not supposed to online, do you?"

"Are you asking if I have a place waiting for me at the Black Hat conference in Vegas this year?"

"...is that like the Red Hat Society with the old women who wear purple...?"

"Yes," Jasmine said after a long enough pause to make it clear it was very much *not* like that. "If the old women who wear purple are extremely good at coding, it would be just like that."

"Then I guess, yes, I'm asking if you have a place at that conference."

"Absolutely not," Jasmine said. "Those people are way, way, *way* out of my league."

Alis never used the video phone when calling Jasmine during faire, but just this once she wished she had, so she could glare at her twin. "Okay, so I don't know what you're saying, then."

"I'm saying I'm not a world-class hacker."

"Are you a like *country*-class hacker? A state championship class hacker? Are there levels like that? Regional champion? I don't know about any of this!"

"What," Jasmine said with what sounded like patient amusement, "do you want hacked?"

"Is this the kind of thing we should be discussing on a public line?"

"Obviously not, but I can't do it anyway so it doesn't matter!"

"Oh. Well, okay. I guess I was just wondering if we could find out who'd filed the paperwork to buy the land before the bank opens tomorrow. And who signed off on it."

"You want somebody to hack a bank and a town council?"

That sounded much worse than however Alis had been thinking about it in her mind. "No! I mean! I guess so, but no, obviously not, not when you put it like that!"

"That's good, 'cause that would be hella illegal. Sooooo does this mean I should or should not be expecting you to come home tonight?"

"Um. Probably I'll be home. I think Jon's so caught up in this whole weird mess he probably doesn't remember I even exist. Which is fine! It's like his livelihood and stuff." Somehow that didn't make it feel quite fine. It felt like a theatrically tragic disappointment, which was ridiculous enough to let Alis smile some of it away. "Although I might need you to come pick me up, honestly. I'll let you know in a while?"

"If I leave this parking place I will never get it back."

"That's what you said this morning when we went to the diner and that turned out fine!" Alis paused. "Was that only this morning?"

"It's been a busy day, babe. Romantic interludes and getting your ass handed to you by Lord Argent."

Alis groaned. "Did you have to remind me?"

"Yes. I need the fires of vengeance burning in your chest. I did not take two weeks out of my busy schedule for Lord Edward to lose his winning streak to a pompous ass like Argent."

"You didn't take two weeks out of your busy schedule at all," Alis pointed out. "You're a digital nomad."

"Do not bother me with such trifling truths," Jazz said with a sniff. "But do call me if you need me to come pick you up, okay?"

Alis laughed. "Yeah, okay. Thanks, baby sister."

"You're welcome, *old lady*."

Alis went *pthththbbbt* into the phone, and hung up to Jasmine's laughter. Then she lay back on the picnic table, looking up at the stars. She couldn't quite decide if she wanted to go in or not. It was so peaceful out here, and so very, very loud in there. On the other hand, she hated missing whatever might be going on.

"Alis?" Jon's quiet, concerned voice came out of the darkness, from the direction of the beer garden. A thrill of happiness shot through her, warm and comfortable, and she lifted a hand to wave at him.

"Over here, lazing around in the extreme quiet."

Jon laughed as he made his way across the lawn. Alis sat up, and he leaned on the table beside her, smiling ruefully. "Overwhelmed you, did they?"

"Some," she admitted. His body heat was enough to remind her she'd gotten a little chilly. She scooted closer, and he put his arm around her shoulders. Alis thought she might melt. "I also wanted to call my sister and check in."

"That's nice, that you guys have a relationship where you do that. Is it just you two, or...?"

"Oh, no, our parents still live back in Maryland. Jasmine and I are just still in each other's pockets, I guess, even though we're adults now."

"I'm obviously not one to throw stones. Laurie and I are thick as thieves. Anyway, I didn't mean to lose track of you in there, so when Ashley said you'd come outside I just wanted to make sure you were okay."

"I liked Ashley, she's great. And of course I'm fine. But I don't think I'm much help in this situation. You all know the people to call and what to do, so I'm just a weirdo watching from the wings."

"Aaah, no way. You're the main event, as far as I'm concerned. Don't ever forget it."

Alis made a small, startled noise, though she shook her head as Jon glanced down at her. "Just the idea of being the main event. That's funny. My sister and I generally shared the spotlight."

Jon made a face and a reluctant sound. "I guess that's how it should be, right? Parents don't want you to think they've got favorites. My folks were good at that, especially since there were four of us. But with all due respect..." His smile flashed in the darkness. "I'm sure your sister's very nice and everything, but I think it'd be kind of gross if I wanted you to share the spotlight with her as far as *I'm* concerned."

Alis laughed, startled again. "Yeah, it would be. All right. I'll be your main event." For the next seven days, she thought. Seven days wasn't that much time.

Seven days *wasn't* that much time, and Alis suddenly felt like she was wasting it. She slipped off the picnic table and caught Jon's hand, gazing up into his eyes. "Do you have to go back in?"

His eyes widened a little. "I doubt it. It's the middle of the night. Nobody can get any real business done until morning, so they're all in there just shouting about what should be done. They won't miss me."

"Then I think we should get out of here."

Jon stood, all six foot two of him, and smiled down at her. "To anywhere in particular?"

Alis held her breath. "Your place?"

Hope and amusement sparked in his eyes. "You realize that means the high likelihood of facing my brother down in the morning?"

"It's a risk I'm willing to take," Alis promised. "He's got that bad knee. I bet I can take him in a fight, if necessary."

Jon laughed. "I have no doubt you could. C'mon, then, let me take you home."

Alis slipped her hand into his, and they ran for his truck like they were trying to get away with something. Apparently Jon felt that way too, because he actually giggled once they were in the truck. "I feel like I'm sixteen and sneaking out of the house to meet a girl."

"No, no, we're sneaking *in* to the house," Alis pointed out, and Jon laughed again.

"Except we don't have to sneak in. There's nobody home. This is definitely a sneaking-out kind of feeling." It was only about a two minute drive to his house, enough time to send Jasmine a text saying she wouldn't be home after all. She and Jon were still fighting off snickers and giggles when they scurried through the yard and down to Jon's room. He closed the door behind him, leaned on it, and looked down at Alis in sudden concern. "This is okay? We can go up to the kitchen and get some snacks and just hang out, if you want."

She stepped up against him, flattening her palm

against his chest. "Snacks later, maybe. Right now…" She looked him up and down, then smiled hungrily. "Right now I want a *meal*."

His hands slid into her hair and pulled her even closer so he could cover her mouth with his, a devouring kiss that left them both breathless before he murmured, "That was a good line and a great answer. Lights on? Lights off?" He fumbled toward a light switch and Alis caught his hand, smiling.

"I'm a moonlight and shadows kind of girl." Then she glanced toward a window and snickered. "Well, streetlights and shadows. No real moon tonight."

"Streetlights and shadows are good." Jon kissed her throat, sending heat spilling through Alis. His hands were big and certain, warmer than her skin everywhere that he touched her. She shivered under that warmth, feeling goosebumps rise and her nipples harden, and she whimpered, catching his hand again and sliding it over her breast. He ran his thumb over her nipple, then came back to pinch it with just enough strength, making her gasp and sending her building desire into overdrive.

"You liked that," he breathed. Alis whimpered again, lifting her chest into his touch, then catching her breath as he tugged her nipple again. It felt so good, blotting out all thought, making her crave nothing more than to be touched. She felt his other hand at her waist, beneath her tanktop, and he pulled the fabric lightly. "Take it off."

She didn't think she'd ever pulled a shirt off so fast in her life. Jon flicked the fastening of her bra open as the shirt came off, and suddenly his mouth was on her nipple, sucking and nibbling as his fingertips played the other one. Alis thought she should be falling over, or maybe she was flying, bent back, oh, that explained why she wasn't falling. She was bent back in his arm, his easy, confident strength along her spine, holding her in place while he teased her breasts until she was clinging to his hair and whimpering helplessly. Her whole world was made up of the aching pleasure in her nipples and the throbbing heat between her legs, and she couldn't quite figure out if she wanted more immediately or to be deliciously tormented forever.

Jon answered that for her, straightening up just before she thought she might actually come from the attention he'd paid to her swollen nipples. He stripped his shirt off, giving her a glimpse of strong, gorgeous muscle before he turned her away from himself and pressed her against the door. Alis gasped and Jon slid a hand down her belly, beneath her waistband, beneath her panties, and stopped with his fingertips just barely delving into her cleft. Alis cried out impatiently and tipped her hips forward, trying to encourage his touch where she wanted it to be, and felt his grin against her shoulder. "You want it just like that?"

"Please, Jon, yes. Please!"

He pressed against her, the incredible heat of his body warming her from shoulder to ass, then slid his fingers deeper, capturing her clit between them. Alis cried out again, rolling her hips into his touch, and his smile flickered against her shoulder again. "That's right.

Go on, Alis. Take as much as you want. I'm right here. I won't let you fall."

She didn't think she *could* fall, with his fingers so deep between her thighs, with his hand trapped so close against her thanks to the shorts he still hadn't removed. She gasped something, half a protest, half pleading, a little embarrassed at how badly she wanted to ride his fingers until she came. Then he lifted his free hand to her breast again, pinching and tugging her nipple with the same rough care as before, and her embarrassment fled in a desperate need to get off on the strong fingers working between her legs.

Orgasm hit like a gift from above, white-hot pleasure that soaked her shorts and left her too wobbly to stand. Not that she was in any danger of falling, with Jon's arm around her so snugly as he crooned approval but shuddered with desire of his own. "Alis, can I…?"

"God, please, yes! Condom," she added a little hazily, and he breathed a laugh that spilled cool air down her spine.

"Got one." He kept his fingers lodged between her legs, letting her moan and move against them as he finally unzipped her shorts and pushed them down. His own jeans went the same way, followed by a faintly frustrated laugh. "Getting this on is a two-hand job. Hang on."

Still a little vaguely, she said, "I can help," and started to turn, but he leaned into her again, his hot length pressing against her ass.

"You stay right where you are."

Alis made a noise, thin and high and helpless as the

command shivered through her, then moaned as his hand slipped away from between her legs so he could put the damned condom on. Then he leaned up against her again, the scent of latex faint in the air as he put his hand over her cleft again, the same not-quite-there touch as before. "Is like this okay?"

"Anything's okay! Please, I want it!"

Jon laughed and kissed her shoulder. "I want you so much. You're so damn beautiful."

"I'm here. I'm here, please, Jon, God, take me, I'm here!" Alis couldn't remember ever begging like this before, but the man behind her was so strong and certain, and being with him felt so right that it was all she ever wanted to do. She pushed her hips back into his, whimpering, then groaned out loud as he slid his fingers over her clit again. For a moment she was at war with herself, wanting to press back so he would claim her and wanting to press forward and ride his fingers again. But then he tilted her hips for her, and took her deeply, his cock sliding beautifully over the sensitive spot inside as his fingers squeezed her clit again. Alis said, "Oh my God," thickly. "Oh my God, yes, Jon, yes, holy—!" and came a second time.

He breathed, "Oh *yeah*," against her spine and held still a moment, pressing deep inside her with a mind-blowing breadth, shuddering with pleasure at *her* pleasure. "That's my girl. That's good. God, Alis, you feel good." He withdrew slowly and pushed back in again just as slowly, murmuring praise until Alis began to claw at the door and at his hip, pleading for more. Then she felt his smile again, and heard a murmured,

"You want it quick and dirty, is that it, Alis? You want to not know what hit you?"

"Yes! God, yes, hard and fast and then, *then* slow, okay, Jon? Please? Yes? Please, I want to feel you come, too, it'll be so hot and good." Alis didn't know what she'd done with herself, asking for that, but it felt right in the moment, and it felt even better as Jon groaned and thrust into her harder.

"I won't last," he said thickly. "If I go fast, Alis, I won't last."

She grabbed his hip again, pushing herself back onto him. "That's kind of the idea, yes, please, please?"

He whispered, "Oh, God," against her shoulder, then drove into her hard enough to cross her eyes in the best possible way. She braced, pushing back, lost in the heat and passion, and cried out with him as Jon's heat spilled in deep throbs that were exactly, *exactly* what she wanted to feel.

They stood together for a few seconds in the aftermath, and Alis didn't know whose knees buckled first, only that they were suddenly on the floor in a giggling, gasping tangle, seeking each other's mouths for kisses and nuzzles, and that it was perfect.

CHAPTER 13

Sunlight slid across Alis's face like another warm nuzzle, making her smile and throw her arm over her eyes drowsily. She had no idea what time it was. She didn't care. The only time she and Jon had moved more than an arm's length apart all night was when Jon had gone to throw her clothes into the washing machine, and then the dryer, which Alis really, *really* appreciated, because they were absolutely not going to be fit for wear otherwise.

He'd picked her up last night, when they'd gotten off the floor. She was much too tall for men to pick her up, generally, but he'd done it easily, and carried her to the bed like it was nothing. He'd sat her on the edge of it, knelt, and had worked his way down her body with his mouth, driving her to a frenzy of need she wouldn't have thought possible as he kept that 'fast, then slow' promise in spades.

Unfortunately, instead of being able to stay there and explore that some more, nature called. Alis groaned and rolled out of bed, lurching toward the bathroom as she heard Jon roll over behind her. Then he audibly sat up and said, "Oh my *God.* What happened to you? I didn't do that!" in real horror.

Alis sleepily looked down, turning around like she could see her whole self better that way, but there wasn't anything amiss, as far as she could tell. "Um?"

"That *bruise!*" Jon scooted to the edge of the bed and lifted her arm. Alis peered, then pulled her boob inward with the opposite hand so she could more easily see past it to her ribs.

There was a *massively* impressive purple bruise from where she'd taken the hit from Lord Argent in their exhibition bout. It was about the length of her hand and most of an inch wide, wrapping around her ribs. She blinked at it, then at Jon. "Sword fighting?"

"Sw—you fight?"

"I spar," Alis said cautiously. It felt absurd to keep the Black Knight's secret from him, but she'd been keeping it so long in general that it also felt impossible to confess now. "I probably picked it up during a session and didn't notice."

Jon spluttered, but dropped her arm. "How do you not notice a bruise like that?"

"Well." Alis let her boob go and lifted her arm again, demonstrating with a gesture how it got in the way of her line of sight. "And I've been on the road, staying in an RV with a bathroom mirror about the size of a nickel, so I didn't see it in my reflection."

"But bruises hurt!"

Alis couldn't stop herself from prodding the bruise,

which of course hurt, which made her laugh. "Yeah, but how often do you poke yourself in the ribs? And it's right below where my bra sits, so the band doesn't put pressure on it. And..." She shrugged. "Sparring is how I get most of my exercise. You get used to bruises from it and kind of stop noticing, you know?" She twisted, trying to get a better look at the rest of herself. "I probably have others. Yeah, my calf, my hip there..."

Those ones were older and less horrible, because she *did* spar a lot, and hadn't taken any meaningful hits three days ago in those places. Poor Jon still looked horrified, even when she gave him an apologetic smile. "I'm okay, really. Sorry to freak you out."

Jon shook his head and put his hand out for hers. Alis took it, letting him reel her in and press his forehead against her breastbone as his hands slid to her waist, big and strong and confident. His breath spilled down her belly, warming her, before he gave an embarrassed chuckle. "I have this overwhelming compulsion to keep you safe," he said against her skin. "Seeing a bruise like that lit up all the 'grr, argh' parts of my brain. Sorry if I got a little intense."

Alis laughed quietly and tilted his chin up with both her hands so she could bend and steal a soft kiss. "I can take care of myself, but thanks for the thought."

"I don't doubt it, but..." Jon took a deep breath and sighed it out. "There's something I should probably have mentioned earlier, but it's hard to explain in words. But it has to do with that compulsion to take care of you."

"Compulsion, that's a weird word, like I have you

enthralled." Alis made woo-woo fingers, wiggling them at Jon, who laughed, started to speak again, and was drowned out by Alis's phone. "That's Jasmine's ring, I better get it."

"That's fine." He fell back into bed, folding his arms behind his head to watch her. Alis usually felt self-conscious being watched when she was naked, but Jon's little pleased smile made her feel rather strong and powerful. She found the phone on the floor beneath her shorts and answered, trying to sound normal.

"Hey, Jazz, what's up?"

"Oh my God, you *did* get laid. You sound like the cat who stole the canary."

Alis felt a blush starting somewhere around her ribcage and hid her face in one hand. "That is none of your business. Also, what did you think I was going to do?"

"I thought you might chicken out. You're not really the one night stand twin. Anyway, you can tell me all the details later. I wanted you to know the guy who signed off on the fairground sale is a Chester Whitfield. The town mayor, apparently."

"Oh my God. Does he like dressing in baby clothes and being spanked?"

Jasmine screeched a horrified, "*What?*" in her ear as Jon crunched up, suddenly alert.

"No, nothing, it was a joke, but—how did you find that out? Why did he sign off? Does sign off mean the sale has gone through, or just that it's been approved by the town?"

"I don't know why, but the last part. It's been approved by the town, in the form of the mayor. There's a bunch of other legal stuff that's supposed to go down at the bank before the actual sale goes through."

"Jazz." Alis wobbled back to the bed and put the phone on speaker. "I'm putting you on speaker so Jon can hear this too. Jon, this is my sister Jasmine."

"Hi, Jasmine. Nice to meet you. Sort of."

"It's sort of nice to meet me?" Jasmine sounded properly indignant, and Alis, trying to untangle her bra, giggled.

"It's nice to sort of meet you!" Jon said, equally indignant at her misinterpretation.

This, Alis thought, was going *great*. They would smart-ass each other to death if she gave them the chance. "Jazz! Focus! How did you find this out?"

"Just because I don't wear purple and red together doesn't mean I don't know people who do," Jasmine said cryptically.

Jon blinked at Alis, befuddled, and she groaned. "Oh. I see. I'll explain when we're off the phone," she said to Jon, whose expression relaxed into acceptance. "Did anybody else sign off on the sale, Jazz?"

"Not as far as I can tell. Does the mayor even have the power to do that?"

Alis exhaled loudly. "According to Jon's brother, yeah, he does."

"Is his brother a lawyer?"

"No, but he is a busybody," Jon said. "And he must be right, because if the mayor doesn't actually have the power, the sale wouldn't be legal, so all of this subterfuge would be pointless."

"Unless the buyer is counting on possession being nine-tenths of the law," Jasmine said. "I bet they could tie it up in court for ages, anyway."

"Do you know who the buyer is?" Alis asked hopefully.

She could almost hear her sister shake her head. "No, sorry, my ladies in purple haven't found that information yet."

Jon mouthed, "'Ladies in purple?'" and Alis waved it off, again promising the explanation in a minute.

"Let me know if they do, I guess?"

"Yep, I will. Jon, you better have been good, because I'm going to be nagging Al for all the details." Jasmine hung up as Alis blushed again.

"I swear I have no intention of giving her the details," Alis promised.

Jon *also* blushed, which made her feel better. "As long as you don't let her think it wasn't worth sharing them." He suddenly looked worried. "It was, wasn't it?"

"Oh my God." Alis leaned over to kiss him. "It was *so* worth sharing them, but I'm still not going to. And if we didn't go have a mayor to find and question, I'd prove it to you."

"Mayor Whitfield!" Jon stopped blushing in favor of looking baffled. "What the hell was he thinking? We'll go find out, but I'm showering first. We're showering first?" he asked hopefully.

"That will not get us out of here in a timely fashion," Alis warned. At Jon's fallen expression, she grinned. "I didn't say no, just that it wouldn't get us out of here fast. Especially because I get the impression you *like* slow."

Jon closed in on her, sliding his arms around her waist. "Come shower with me and find out."

He definitely liked slow, Alis concluded a while later. That, and he was incredibly creative with shower head settings. She was never going to leave his house at this rate, although by that time she was starving and even more grateful that he'd washed her clothes, which he went to get while still wearing only a towel.

Better yet, he came back still only wearing a towel. Or two: one around his hips, and the other around his hair. Alis, presented with about seven acres of broad, muscled man chest, temporarily forgot how to put her clothes on anyway. "Wow. You could wear that all day, as far as I'm concerned."

"Towels aren't known for their stability," Jon told her. "You probably don't want me to flash half the faire while I'm serving drinks."

"I mean…the risk might be worth it?" Especially with the way curls trailed down his lower belly to disappear under the towel. Alis thought it might *definitely* be worth it. "You're incredibly gorgeous. You know that, right?"

He gave her a crooked grin. "I have moments where I think I'm all right." He dropped the towel around his hair, ran a pick through it to loosen the strands, and then with incredible deftness, flicked his hair into a series of tiny Viking-style braids that he then bound together into one bigger one.

Alis watched the entire process with awe. "I can barely comb my own hair, compared to that. Holy crap, dude."

"You've got all those curls," he said sympathetically. "I haven't worked with curly hair much, but it seems harder. Curl patterns and everything. But I can braid yours sometime if you want."

"My God, and to think I wasted all that time last night having great sex when I could have gotten my *hair braided.*" Alis was only half kidding. "I would love that. I've always wanted those Viking-style braids but there's no way I can do them myself."

"It's really easy on somebody else," Jon promised. "Maybe after you get that shower and we've figured out this whole mayor thing. What the hell could Whitfield be thinking?" he asked again, as if Alis might have come up with an answer while they were in the shower.

"No idea. I haven't exactly been thinking about Whitfield for the last half hour."

"I mean, I'm glad to hear that. Oh! Wait! What was that about women in red and purple?"

Alis laughed. "Oh, right. Do you know that poem? 'When I am old, I shall wear purple?'" At the shake of his head, she said, "It's a poem about a woman getting older and how she'll wear purple and a red hat that doesn't go with the purple. And I guess there are hackers who also wear red hats, or something? So it turns out my sister knows some of them and that's why she told me she got it from the ladies in red and purple."

Jon had stopped getting dressed as she explained,

and just stood there, a t-shirt in his hands and a funny little smile on his face. "I'm so glad I asked. No, I mean that. It's completely nutty and I love it. So, um, do you want to go back to your RV and shower first, or... there's a great bakery nearby we could go to for breakfast?"

"Oh, breakfast first." Alis had to text Jasmine to get her out of the RV anyway, if she was going back to it with Jon. Or she could tell him the truth about Lord Edward, but she'd kept the secret for so damn long. Besides, she only had to keep up this double life for another week here in Renaissance, and then she'd be gone and all of this would be a fond memory anyway.

For some reason that sent a pang through her heart that took her breath away. Or maybe that was watching Jon finish getting dressed, because that, too, was certainly pang-worthy. Those denim shorts fit that fine ass like a glove, and his t-shirt clung to his body like it was afraid he'd get away.

Or maybe Alis was afraid he'd get away, but that was a silly thought.

Jon came to offer her a hand up from the bed, a crooked smile in place. "Tell me how you're feeling about the high likelihood of running into my brother out there. Is this walk of shame territory?"

"Oh, believe me, you have *nothing* to be ashamed of." Alis grinned and let him pull her to her feet, standing on her toes to steal a kiss. "And if he's the kind of ass who thinks he'll shame *me*, he's got another think coming."

"No, actually." Jon's eyebrows went up a little, as if

surprised by the thought. "I don't think he'd try that at all. Not under the circumstances, anyway."

"What circumstances? The one where I maybe accidentally helped save the Faire?" Alis smiled.

"Um." Jon squinted. "Yeah, we'll go with that for the moment. I meant to explain something to you, but—"

"Jon!" Laurie's tenor bellowed through the house. "If you don't get out here I'm gonna eat all these cinnamon rolls!"

"Oh, he didn't." Jon's eyes widened hopefully and tugged Alis toward the door. As soon as it opened, the scent of cinnamon and sweet frosting rolled into the room. Alis's stomach grumbled and Jon flashed her a grin. "You have no idea. You'll be glad you're a two-breakfast kind of woman."

Alis gave a laugh of dismay as she scurried up the stairs after Jon. Maybe she could explain she only ate two peoples' worth of breakfast once a week. For some reason she didn't want to disappoint him.

It was a nice house, split-level entry, bedrooms to the left upstairs and to the right downstairs, with upstairs and downstairs living rooms on opposite sides, and the kitchen/dining room off the upstairs living room. Alis had only gotten a glimpse of it last night, and now that she was seeing it more clearly, she still thought it had been decorated by Jon's mom: it didn't look like a bachelor pad at all.

And the box of enormous cinnamon rolls on the dining room table didn't look like they were home-made, but they did look absolutely delicious. Alis considered the possibility she *could* eat two peoples' worth of breakfast. "Oh my God. Those are huge."

"Literally as big as your face," Laurie said as he got milk and juice out of the fridge. He looked perky, like he'd been up a while, and also terribly pleased with himself.

"Sometimes," Jon informed his brother, "you don't suck."

"That's a terrible way to say thank you." Laurie sniffed.

Alis, enthusiastically, said, "*Thank* you, Laurie. Where did you get these?"

"The bakery I was going to take you to." Jon held Alis's chair for her, which was a cute, funny, charming, old-fashioned thing to do, especially at his own breakfast table. "You have to get there early to get them, though. They usually sell out before ten."

"Which," Laurie said modestly, "is why I went to get some at eight. They should still be warm."

"They must be," Alis said. "They smell incredible."

Jon served one to her, which was a polite way of saying he shoveled it onto the plate, but with the amount of brown-sugar caramel and cream cheese frosting dripping from it, 'shovel' was the only way it was going to get from the box into her belly. Alis immediately tore a piece off with her fingers, ate it, and groaned. "Oh, that's amazing. Oh my God. That does it, I'm moving to Renaissance. Do you need school teachers?"

Laurie shot Jon a *Look*, and Jon shot him a clearly warning one back. Alis had no idea what that byplay was about, but as long as she had the cinnamon roll, she didn't care. She spent a few happy minutes stuffing her face, only slowing down as she reached the center of the roll, which was still hot enough to scorch her fingers. She licked them, but wasn't about to let a little heat keep her from finishing the best cinnamon roll of her life. "On second thought, I'd never stop eating these if I lived here. You guys must live at that bakery."

"We usually do a Sunday morning breakfast at the pub," Jon admitted. "However much of the family wants to show up, does, and we eat these things and catch up on the gossip for the week."

"Aw. That sounds great!"

"It is. And it keeps us from eating our body weights in cinnamon rolls the rest of the week, because we know we've got them to look forward to."

"Says you," Laurie objected.

"Okay, it keeps *most* of us from eating our body weight in cinnamon rolls the rest of the week. What'd you guys decide last night after we left? Did we miss anything?"

Laurie shook his head while Alis nabbed a second cinnamon roll. She couldn't possibly eat it all, but she was by god going to try. "Well, we got a hit this morning. Do you know the mayor?"

"I've met him. Why? Wait, no way. Is he behind this?"

"Looks like maybe, yeah. I think Jon and I were going to go pay him a visit this morning. Did you want to come along? Actually, no, what am I thinking. It would make way more sense for you two to go see him while I go home and get ready for Faire. For a minute I forgot this isn't actually my business." Another pang of longing struck Alis, but she took a deep breath, trying to chase it away.

She thought Jon looked sad for a moment, but then he smiled reassuringly. "That sounds like it might be a plan. Ow!" The last part was because Laurie had clearly kicked him under the table. Jon glared at his brother. "It's a *plan*, Laurie."

Alis grimaced, not knowing what she'd gotten in between, then offered an awkward smile. "Know what, I think I'll call a taxi to to bring me back to the fairgrounds. Seems like there's a lot for you guys to do, and the faire does still open at eleven this morning, after all."

She grabbed her cinnamon roll and fled.

CHAPTER 14

"Dude! What'd you let her go for? Haven't you told her about being mates yet? This is all her business! Everything in Renaissan—ow!" Laurie pulled his leg up, looking injured as Jon glared at him across the table.

"I haven't told her anything."

"Well, go tell her! She's probably still waiting for the taxi!" Laurie jumped up to go check, and Jon was tempted to trip his brother. But that would end up with a bear wrestling match in the living room—he knew this from experience—and their mother would somehow *teleport* up from Arizona to yell at them. Jon was sure of it. So instead of tripping Laurie, he just sighed and put his face in his hands.

"You heard her, though, Laur. She's got a life somewhere else."

"And she's willing to give it all up for these cinnamon rolls!"

"Oh, come on. That's just something people say. They don't mean it."

Laurie returned from the window looking sullen. "She walked down the street or something. Or the taxi was really fast. She's not there, anyway. Dude, you can't let her go, she's your mate!"

"Yeah, unless the Black Knight is!"

"Haven't you talked to *him* yet either?" Laurie sat back down at the table with his cinnamon roll, but also threw his hands in the air. "What are you wasting time for? And why does it have to be one or the other?"

"Because *every* time I see Lord Edward I get that feeling of it being right, but it only happens sometimes with Alis. Maybe I'm supposed to choose."

Laurie's expression turned sympathetic. "That sounds lousy, dude. But, I don't know, Alis stayed here last night. Doesn't that mean you chose her?"

"But she must have a choice, too, right?" Jon asked dully. "And she just said none of this was her business."

"I swear to God, I'm gonna drown you in a cinnamon roll," Laurie said. "You're gonna have to use your words, Jon. You're going to have to explain every-thing, and if *then* she chooses to leave, well, at least you tried. But you can't just sit here hoping it'll all work out and moping when it doesn't if you haven't actually talked to the woman about it."

"Yeah, well, since when do you know anything about women?" Jon backed that up hastily, raising his hands against Laurie's smirk. "About relationships."

"Okay, fine, relationships aren't my strong suit. But you know I'm right. You've got to talk to her and the Black Knight."

"I know. But right *now* I have to go find out why Mayor Whitfield is trying to sell off the fairgrounds!"

"Half the family is on that, Jon. Uncle Dave is looking into secret real estate agent databases about what's been listed for sale and—"

Jon eyed him. "'Secret real estate databases?'"

"You know, whatever. They've gotta have something like that, don't they? And Mac is filing an injunction against the sale, however that works. What do you think *you're* gonna accomplish that they can't?"

"Talking to the mayor," Jon said patiently. "Because Dave and Mac are *busy*, see."

"I could talk to the mayor. You should go throw yourself at Alis's feet and beg her to stay with you forever."

Yes, Jon's bear said enthusiastically. *Let's do that.*

Jon set his jaw, feeling a counterproductive stubbornness setting in. "I don't need everybody nagging me."

"Hah! Your bear said I was right, didn't it? See? You should listen to your little brother for once!"

"*Enough*, Laurie!" Jon stood abruptly and, grabbing his wallet and keys, left the house without saying anything else. He had a week left with Alis. It had to be enough time to work things out. Enough time to find the Black Knight and talk to him, too, to try to figure out what that electric connection between them meant.

But if all of that was fate, then it meant it *would* work out, somehow. The sale of the fairgrounds wasn't fate at all, which meant it could go really badly. Not just for Jon personally, but for the whole town. For all the vendors across the whole western United States who came to sell their work at the faire. It could take years to get into another one, the wait lists were so long. Losing this one would be devastating to every single community Jon was part of.

And he could think of no earthly reason that Mayor Whitfield would threaten that. He wasn't a shifter, so he couldn't be facing pressure from that front. Jon obviously knew nothing about the man's finances, but being a mayor probably paid pretty well. Maybe not all the money in the world, but enough, surely. He swung up into his truck and looked up the salary, then stared at his phone a minute. It was about a third of what he'd expected, not really even enough to live on, and Whitfield had a family. Maybe Jon could understand an attempt to get rich quick after all, even if it was at the town's expense.

Although the land wasn't Whitworth's to sell, so any profit he'd make would be through a kickback or an outright bribe. If it was Jon in that position, it would have to be a hell of a lot of money to see him through the sleepless nights that would follow. He pulled out of the driveway and guided the truck down the street, only to pass Alis resolutely stalking down the sidewalk toward the middle of town. Jon pulled over and rolled the window down, leaning out to peer at her as she approached. "Everything okay?"

"I don't know, is it? You guys got weird back there and I thought I should dip. But it turns out this town has two taxis and no rideshare services. How do you even live like that? Barbarians!" She didn't sound serious at the end of it.

Jon tilted his head toward the passenger seat. "Well, you can share my ride if you'd like. There are no rideshares here because of our traffic laws. A bunch of local persnicketiness that makes trying to run one more work than it's worth."

Alis stopped outside the driver's door and looked up at him, arms folded beneath her breasts. "Persnicketiness, huh? That's a word that doesn't get a lot of air time."

"Just don't ask me to spell it." Jon smiled hopefully. "I'll drive you to your RV, if you want. Or to the mayor's office, if you want to come with me. I know you said it isn't your business, but…I guess I hope you'll change your mind about that."

Alis glanced down the road indecisively. "I don't know. How long do you think talking to the mayor is going to take?"

"You'll have plenty of time to get back to the fairgrounds and change before the gates open," Jon promised. "At the very least let me take you to the taxi rank in town."

"Where all two taxis are?" Alis asked wryly, but finally came around the truck to climb in. "I know this isn't a big town, but two taxis can't possibly be enough."

"There are two taxi *companies*," Jon said. "There are more actual taxis. And it's probably not enough, but most people here drive. Unless you're right downtown everything's too spread out to walk to most places."

"Basically the story of the entire United States," Alis

said. "All right, let's try the mayor's office before you drop me at the taxi rank. Is he even going to be in?" She checked her phone as Jon glanced at the dashboard clock. It was just about eight-thirty, although the sun was far enough up to make it seem later: the heat was coming on, and shadows had firmed up, no longer soft and stretched with sunrise.

"He should be, yeah. Most places around here get started by eight. Earlier if it's the bakery or a coffee shop."

"That bakery must start baking at two a.m.," Alis said, suddenly bright-eyed. "They must be beating people off with a stick by six. I would *live* there."

"They stay incredibly busy," Jon agreed. "In the winter, people staying up at the lodges come down off the mountain just to get breakfast there, and in the summer the faire keeps them hopping." Worry sluiced through him again. The bakery was yet another busi-ness that couldn't afford to lose the faire. Aloud, not meaning to, he murmured, "What the hell was Whit-field thinking?"

Alis reached over to put a sympathetic hand on his thigh. It was warm, reassuring, and slightly distracting. "Maybe there will turn out to be a good reason. Maybe it's just somebody who wants to develop more perma-nent structures in the fairgrounds. Extra bathrooms or something."

Jon gave her a quick glance and sighed. "We *could* use more bathrooms."

"See?" Alis said with a hopeful smile. "It could all be innocuous. A nice surprise."

"Do you believe that?"

"No." Alis shrugged. "But you have to take a positive attitude to survive teaching third graders, so I try to apply that to other aspects of my life."

Jon hadn't expected to laugh much this morning, but that made him laugh. "I could use a lesson or two in that, maybe. Look, Alis, there's something I want to talk to you about."

She glanced at him, looking slightly defensive. "Is this the 'this can only be temporary, a faire affair' talk? I *am* aware that I'm leaving in a week, Jon."

"What? No! No—oh, God, you don't think I have affairs every faire, do you? You're not just the girl of the week, or the summer, Alis. I really like you."

Go on, his bear said. *Tell her the rest.*

Alis, dryly, said, "I think if I was a six foot two blond with shoulders like yours I would be having affairs as often as I felt like it, yes. Which is fine! But—" She faltered. "I actually really like you, too, but I *am* leaving in a week. I've got two more faires this summer and then I've got to get back to work. I don't see how that would work out, and besides," she said, obviously forcing herself to rally, "we've known each other what, almost three days? It could turn out that in another week we can't stand each other."

"No. No, sometimes you just know." For a heartbeat Jon wanted to tell her everything, about the power of fate and shifters and all of it. In the next heartbeat he had a vision of the Black Knight, his armor swallowing the light as he fought at the fairgrounds, and the words died in his throat.

Tell her! his bear insisted.

Jon shook his head just a little, denying the bear and trying to shake off thoughts of the Black Knight. Neither worked very well. *I am not ready for a discussion about polyamory with a woman I've just met,* he told the bear, and aloud, he repeated, "Sometimes you just know," a little more quietly.

Alis's hand stole back to touch his leg again. "Maybe you're right. But look, let's see what we think at the end of a week, okay? We don't have to make any decisions today."

That was probably the only sensible thing anybody had said in days. Jon cast her a quick smile and nodded, although part of him wanted to tell her that everything was already decided for him. He was going to adore her until the end of time, no matter what.

He just hadn't been prepared to *also* adore Lord Edward.

Jon muffled a groan, and, fortunately, pulled into the city hall parking lot at the same time. Alis put a hand on the door handle, but paused, grinning at the town square. "It's just picture-perfect, isn't it? It looks like an Old West town from the movies."

Jon, halfway out the driver's door, stopped to actually look around, and chuckled. "I guess it kind of does, doesn't it? I don't really see it like that, I guess. It's too familiar."

Alis was right, though. Renaissance's wide Main Street and its town square were lined with stonework buildings, the tallest of which were four stories with their façades, although there were church steeples and government statuary breaking up some of those façades. Jon knew that most of the first-floor businesses had storage rooms or apartments above them, with rent getting cheaper the more flights up somebody had to walk. Three floors wasn't that bad, though. That was the kind of thing he thought about, looking around town. But it *was* pretty, and he liked being reminded of that.

"I don't think I could ever get to where this was familiar," Alis said as she got out of the truck. "It's too spectacular. The mountains backing right up to the town like this?" She put her hand above her eyes, tilting her head back to look beyond the buildings at the Rockies soaring upward in the background. Jon thought that was cute: the sun was behind them and there was absolutely no need to block her eyes.

Alis apparently realized the same thing at the same time and dropped her hand, laughing. "I don't know why I did that. Like a kid pretending to use binoculars, or something, like I could see better that way. But it really is all so intense and gorgeous and vivid. I think it would always take my breath away."

Jon looked up at the stark line of rough mountaintops against the blue morning sky, and smiled. "You're right. I should appreciate it more." His gaze came back to Alis, though, as he murmured, "We should never get used to beauty."

She looked pleased but also rolled her eyes, which made Jon laugh. "I guess that puts me in my place."

"Not your best line," she agreed. "Too cliched. The hatchet face one was much better."

"You're the one who said you had a hatchet face!"

"But you turned it around so well. Which one's the mayor's office?"

"It's in City Hall." Jon offered his hand, and Alis took it as they walked up to the big yellow-brick building with its ornate door. The door usually stood open when the weather permitted, an invitation for anyone to come in and talk to the town government, but this morning it was closed. Not locked, though: Jon pushed it open and stepped inside, squinting briefly as his eyes adjusted to the dimmer light.

Even after they had, it took a moment to understand what he was seeing.

Half the interior doors were broken, either the glass in them shattered or the doors themselves halfway off their hinges, bent and misshapen. There were papers scattered everywhere, and the front counter, a massive thing that had been there since the 1880s, was scarred from some kind of fight. There were score marks across it, the kind of thing a bear or wildcat might make. Jon fought the powerful urge to shift and see if his paws would fit the size of the scarring. He was almost certain they would.

But a bear or wildcat that size couldn't possibly wander through downtown Renaissance unnoticed. Even more to the point, a bear or wildcat that size almost certainly wasn't a true animal. Only shifters got that big, which meant that whatever problems Jon had thought Renaissance was facing, they were suddenly much, much worse.

CHAPTER 15

PICTURE PERFECT DISSOLVED into cinematic carnage, and Alis didn't know what to do about that. Some kind of fight had clearly taken place in the city hall: she could see spatters of blood, dried brown on the scattered paperwork, and staining the floor and walls. Glass and broken wood was everywhere, making the floor treacherous. It looked like a tornado had blown through, smashing everything up and leaving confusion in its wake. There were even railings broken upstairs; the city hall had two floors, with balcony-style walkways in front of the glass-plated doors up there, like some kind of old saloon. Only one or two of the upstairs doors were wrecked, though almost everything downstairs was.

Right in front of her, in the middle of the ground floor, a large, scarred reception counter had a wall behind it, like a free-standing room had been built in the middle of the otherwise-open floorspace. She leaned to the side just a little, following the line of the central room down the length of most of the building, but the blood drew her attention again.

It was rusty brown, dried all the way through. Which meant whatever had happened here, hadn't happened this morning. "Jon?"

The big man with her flinched, then looked toward her with a grim expression. "Alis..."

"What time does City Hall close on Fridays?"

He blinked, obviously not expecting that question, then passed a hand over the braids he'd put into his hair. "Usually six, just like the rest of the week, but it always closes early the weekend Faire begins, so everybody can get out to be part of the festivities. Four o'clock. Maybe as early as three, if it's not a busy day."

Alis wet her lips. "So this could have happened any time from four o'clock on Friday. What time does the bank close?"

"Five." Jon's eyes widened. "Shit. You think somebody forged paperwork?"

"Or forced it." Alis gestured at the mess around them. "We need to call the police."

"I—we—" Jon growled, a startling deep sound that made Alis take a startled step back. "I need to see the security footage, if there is any." He gestured toward the corners, drawing her attention to cameras, then picked his way through the wreckage with grim determination.

Alis followed, confused and cautious. "Shouldn't the police do that?"

"Yes, but...it's complicated, Alis. I'll try to explain in a minute."

The boxed-in central room had a door halfway down it, the word *Security* etched into the still-whole glass plate that made up its upper half. Jon tried the door and grimaced unhappily when it opened. Alis, still following him, saw the bolt had been kicked out, but somebody had still taken the time to close it behind them.

The security room had desks, screens, an air conditioning unit that Alis bet was critical in the summers, and a series of hard drives that had been completely trashed. Most of the screens were black. When she turned one on, it flipped into a blue screen of death rather than show anything from anywhere in the building. Jon swore, said, "Maybe that's good," and swore again.

"Why would it be good?"

"It's—it's not good, but it's...we don't film well anyway, not when we're..." He was clearly talking to himself, mostly muttering while Alis waited for some kind of explanation.

When it didn't appear to be forthcoming, she took her phone out. "I'm calling the police."

"Alis." Jon's attention all came to focus on her, and he put his hand on top of her phone. "Wait."

"Wait for what? Whatever happened here needs to be investigated!"

"Yes, but we need to make sure the right officers come down."

She eyed him suspiciously. "That doesn't sound good, Jon. What do you mean, the *right* officers?"

"No, I know it doesn't, I just...ah, hell. I was trying

to tell you something earlier, and then I thought maybe I didn't have to tell you right *now*, since we've got another week before you leave, but... you saw those marks on the desk outside?"

Alis smiled briefly. "Yeah, they look like claw marks. What's that about? Some kind of old Colorado folk tale about how Davy Crockett wrassled himself a bear and the town made a desk out of the trees they scarred up?"

Jon groaned. "That would be a great story, but no. The reality is maybe less believable. Alis..." He glanced around the little security room and sighed. "You're going to want to back out of the room for this."

"For *what*? Why?"

"Because I'm going to..." Jon grimaced again, then cast his gaze upward, said, "This is *not* how I wanted to do this," and met her eyes. "I'm going to take up a lot of room in here in a minute, and it'll be a little easier on you if you're not squished up in here with me. I think."

She smiled uncertainly. "I kind of like being squished up against you."

"Not in this case. I mean." He looked around a little wildly. "It'd probably be pretty snuggly? But no, no, definitely not right now. You definitely need breathing room on this one. Can you...will you just trust me on this and go into the hall? But leave the door open."

"I'm very confused, but okay, fine." Alis backed out into the hall, bracing the door open on a bit of scrap. "Okay. I'm out. What's going on?"

"Um. God, is this always this hard? Why don't we have classes in how to explain this? Does everybody just—agh. Okay, look, Alis. I'm what's called a shifter. My whole family is. I can change into a bear."

Alis laughed, and halfway through her laugh, Jon changed into a bear.

Not just a bear. A *big* bear. A huge, shaggy, dark blond grizzly bear who in fact filled up the whole security room as he lifted his huge, shaggy, dark blond head to give her what seemed to be an incredibly apologetic look.

Alis's laugh turned into a shriek. She lurched sideways, grabbed the nearest thing that looked heavy, and lifted it, preparing to throw it. A piece of paper stuck to its bottom crinkled at the corner of her eye and she grabbed it, shoved it in her pocket, and hauled the—she checked her hand. She was holding what appeared to be the plinth of some kind of small but sturdy statue. She hauled the plinth farther back, threatening to throw it.

Jon turned back into a man, holding his hands out as if to stop her, his eyes wide and his expression every bit as apologetic as the bear's. "No no no no nonono! Please no! It's just me! I'm just me! Please don't throw things at me!"

"What do you mean you're just you, you just turned into a bear!"

"I know! I know! Just me turns into a bear! It's a family thing! I swear I'm not going to hurt you!"

She hefted the plinth again, warningly. "Do it again."

For some reason she was possibly even more shocked when he did it again. "What!"

The bear looked like it wanted to cry. So did Jon,

when he shifted back to human, his hands still extended and spread in supplication. "There aren't lots of shifters in the world, but there are enough of us. More than you'd think. There are a lot of us, comparatively, in Renaissance."

Alis still wasn't sure she wouldn't throw the plinth. "Are you telling me Renaissance is full of *bear people*? People bears? What even do I call you?"

"Shifters," Jon said again. His whole body was bent toward her like he could help her understand with his intensity. "You call us shifters. And my whole family are bears, but there are a lot of other types of shifters. Big cats. Wolves." A smile pulled at the corner of his mouth. "Partridges."

Alis's arm was starting to quiver from the weight she held. *Stop that*, she told it. She could lift a sword forever. A plinth shouldn't make her shake.

Of course, a sword was balanced very differently from a plinth, but that wasn't what she wanted to be thinking about right now. "*Partridges*? How does that even work? Birds hardly weigh anything." Her eyebrows drew in tightly enough to start giving herself a headache. "And bears are much bigger than people. How did you even—and where did your *clothes* go?"

"Magic," Jon said, hands still extended. "It's just the magic. I don't know how it works. I just know that it does. Could you please put that thing down?"

"Are you telling me," Alis said, putting it together without quite thinking it through, "are you telling me that those scars on the desk out there were caused by a, a *shifter*?"

"*Yes*," Jon said desperately. "I mean, I think so, which means Renaissance is in some kind of trouble I don't understand, and if we get the wrong authorities involved, it's going to get much, much worse."

Alis slowly lowered the plinth, then let it fall to the floor with a crash, and sighed. "Well, then, I guess we'd better get the *right* authorities involved."

She thought Jon might melt through the floor with relief. For a moment it looked like all his bones had turned to jelly. Well, that was only fair enough, because hers had when he turned into a bear six feet away from her. "All of you?" she added a little faintly.

Jon took a deep breath. "My whole family, yeah."

"And here I told Ashley I thought all of you big friendly blonds were *golden retrievers*."

Jon smiled hopefully. "No. Not golden retrievers, no."

"That's what she said! No wonder she thought it was funny!" Alis hesitated. "Could you…could you do it again one more time?"

His expression softened. "Yeah, of course. Anything you want." He stepped back a little, like he thought she needed more room—and he might have been right—and then shifted again, a huge shaggy bear gazing soulfully at her from the security room.

Alis held herself very still for a moment, then stepped forward, cautiously offering the back of her hand, like she would with a dog. Jon *whuffed*, which she guessed might be like a bear's laugh, and put his nose under her hand. She curled her fingers in the short fur there, astonished at how thick it was, and how soft it *wasn't.* Rough, stiff, protective, more than soft. Heart hammering, she scritched her way up his nose into the short thick fur on his head, which was deep enough to sink her fingers into.

His skull was *huge.* Even with her hand spread all the way out, it barely encompassed half of the bear's head, not even reaching from ear to ear. He did tilt his head into it, though, and Alis could tell he was being careful not to lean too hard. Even so she had to brace herself against the weight, but she gave the top of his head a good scratching and the bear—Jon—rumbled with contentment.

"God. Good thing I know you're happy," she said. "That would be a terrifying sound to come across otherwise."

The bear cocked his head to look up at her apologetically again. Not all that far up, really. His head was about at her collarbones. Alis was stricken by the sudden urge to push his lip back and look at his teeth, so she did, and Jon's expression went from apologetic to indignant.

Alis was fairly certain hers went from curious to 'oh god I wish I hadn't done that.' His teeth were massive. She tilted sideways a bit to look down at his feet, and gave a high-pitched laugh. His claws were even bigger. Or equally big. She didn't know how bear teeth and claws worked out, proportionally. It didn't matter, because either way, they were really big. "Okay," she said faintly. "I think I'm...I'm good now..."

Jon shifted back, and somehow she was pressed right up against him, her fingers still in his hair. Eyes wide, she said, "No offense, but I think I like you better this way."

"That's fine," he said with a smile. "I spend way more time as a human anyway. Are you okay?" His eyebrows drew down with concern. "This wasn't how I wanted to tell you."

"How *did* you want to tell me?"

"I…" Jon screwed his face up and shrugged. "I don't know. Not at a crime scene, anyway. Like, I'm not sure there's a romantic way to say 'hey, by the way, I'm also a bear,' but…this is definitely not it, if there is."

Alis couldn't help a quick laugh. "No, I guess there might not be a great way to do it. Okay, well, does this mean…" She disentangled herself, because it was somewhat difficult to think when pressed all up against Jon's body like that. "Does this mean the 'right' authorities are also shifters? How do you run a town with shifters in it if the police don't all know?"

Jon sighed. "Carefully. There *are* true humans who know about us and help us keep our secrets, and it helps that it's…"

"Not very believable?"

Jon shrugged agreeably. "Basically, yeah. You wouldn't have believed me if I hadn't shown you, and we don't usually go around showing people, so…we're kind of like cryptids. Some people know the truth, others suspect it but everybody thinks they're crazy, and most people don't know at all."

"That must be a hard way to live," Alis said with a sudden burst of sympathy.

"It's not, mostly. Mostly it's great, honestly. Especially in a big family like mine, where we can all just be comfortable with each other and go honey-hunting together."

"I pity the beehives!"

"It's much easier to go to the farmer's market and buy a jar!"

Alis laughed, completely taken by surprise. "Is that what you usually do?"

"Obviously!"

"Well, I know what I'm getting you for Christmas!" Alis looked around and sighed. "Right after we figure out what's going on *now*."

CHAPTER 16

Our mate will be with us at Christmas, Jon's bear said happily. *She wants to stay.*

Jon wanted to believe it was as simple as that, but had to shake his head at the bear. *That's just a thing people say. It doesn't mean anything.*

The bear looked skeptical, but didn't argue. Jon was grateful: he wasn't sure he could handle solving a crime and arguing with his bear at the same time. As it was, he and Alis returned to the front room of the city hall, both of them gazing around in dismay. "There was obviously a fight," Alis said quietly. "You think it was between shifters?"

"I don't know. As far as I know, the mayor is a true human." Which meant there could have been a murder, not just a fight. But he didn't want to say that aloud. "We should ask if anybody has seen him since Friday afternoon, anyway."

As he spoke, the front door, which had closed behind them, swept open again. Hope leaped in his heart, but a woman came through, took one look around, screamed, and ran out again. A few seconds later Jon heard her on the phone, calling the police and saying the culprits were still inside. Alis immediately grabbed her phone and called 911, too, her voice shaking with real emotion as she said, "My friend and I just walked into City Hall and it's been robbed? I don't know, but it's a mess and nobody's here and I think there's blood? No, I'm not from here. My friend is, Jon Torben? My name is Alis Capellas, I'm with the faire. Jon and I came over to talk to the mayor this morning but he's not here—"

Jon could hear the dispatcher's voice sharpen at his name. Hopefully that meant they knew he was a shifter and would send somebody who knew about Renaissance's secret community. Alis was still talking, her voice getting faster and more panicked. "—looks like a wild animal scratched things up? Are there wild animals running around Renaissance? I'm from Bethesda! The biggest animals we have are deer and raccoons! They don't scratch up hardwood!"

Now the dispatcher was calming Alis down. She winked at Jon while he cast one more glance at the dead security cameras, then tilted his head toward the door. Alis went to watch it, pushing it most of the way closed, and Jon took a few seconds to shift and compare the claw marks on the reception counter to his own paw.

His paws were considerably larger. That meant the other shifter probably wasn't a bear.

His bear's nose twitched as it inhaled deeply. *Can't tell,* it said. *Smells funny.*

Jon shifted back to human, asking, *Funny how?*

The bear's nose was still twitching, like a sneeze captured inside Jon's mind. *Funny like wrong,* it said. *I don't like it.*

Could you smell anything else? Jon asked hopefully. *The mayor?* His own shifter-enhanced senses were considerably better than the average human's, but he had nothing on his bear's ability to scent.

It grumbled. *Shift back. Let me smell more.*

I don't know if that's safe, buddy..."Alis? Can you guard the door another minute?"

She was off the phone by then, although she now had it pressed against her chest like it was an old-fashioned wall phone that muffled the sound that way. "Yeah, but be quick. I don't think that woman is coming back in but I can already hear the sirens."

Renaissance wasn't that big a town, and the police station was only a block over from the city hall. Jon was surprised the cops weren't just running over on foot, but since they weren't, he hurriedly shifted again and paced carefully around the torn-up ground floor, trying to avoid glass, debris, and shedding any of his own fur into the mess. He sniffed at the blood, but had no idea whose it was: it smelled like blood, not a person. Otherwise, he could scent the faint lingering aftermath of the Mayor's aftershave, but it was days old, as was every other smell in the room except his own and Alis's.

That was something, at least. He shifted back to

human as Alis made a warning sound, and a few seconds later, four police officers spilled into the city hall. They all had guns out, which was much worse than Jon expected. One was a shifter, at least: a square-jawed guy named Gus who had graduated a few years ahead of Jon's older brothers.

Gus barked for them to put their hands up, and they both did, while the woman who'd called from outdoors hopped around and shouted, "That's them! They're the ones I saw in here! They've been in there all morning!"

Alis gave the officers a shaky smile. "We've been in here about five minutes. I called 911 a few minutes ago."

Gus nodded. "Your call came in at the same time hers did. If you've been here five minutes, why didn't you call five minutes ago?"

"Because the first thing we thought was to check to see if anybody was still here and hurt," Alis said. "We didn't check upstairs, though. I was afraid someone might still be there."

Gus's gaze flickered to Jon, who nodded. The officer sighed and holstered his weapon, gesturing for them to put their hands down. "Hi, Jon. Sorry about the guns. Did you see anything useful? Check the upstairs, guys." That was to the other officers, who spread out and began going upstairs.

"What look like claw marks on the reception desk," Jon said quietly. "Blood. All the stuff your men will see. But what you don't know is that late Friday afternoon—"

"Somebody filed paperwork to start the process of

selling the fairgrounds? The whole town's talking about it." Gus crooked a smile as Jon blinked with surprise.

"Word gets around fast. Well, okay, but did you know it has Whitfield's signature on it?"

Gus's ready smile fell away, leaving a serious, good-looking man with worried light blue eyes. "I did not know that. And he's not in?" He pinched a radio on his shoulder, saying, "Somebody go check the mayor's house and let me know if he's all right," before releasing it.

"I thought maybe he was trying to make a buck for himself," Jon admitted. "But then we got here this morning and it all looks a lot more desperate than that."

"So you were coming over to confront him?" Gus squinted. "How did *you* know his signature was on the paperwork?"

This, Jon thought with sudden clarity, is why you were supposed to never talk to the cops. He couldn't answer without getting *somebody* in trouble.

"We found this," Alis answered. She stepped up with an old-fashioned piece of carbon paper, something Jon hadn't seen since he was a kid. He'd forgotten they even existed. It had handwriting pressed into it, hurried cursive scribbles authorizing the release of the fairgrounds for sale. It was signed by the mayor, and dated the previous Friday. "Sorry. I realized too late that I shouldn't have picked it up, but Jon hasn't touched it, so you can take my fingerprints to eliminate them. Hopefully it'll have the mayor's and whoever did this."

Gus pulled a pair of gloves out of his pocket and put one on before he took the paper, eyeing first Jon, then Alis. "When exactly did you find this?"

"When we were looking to see if anyone was hurt. I hadn't seen carbon paper in so long I picked it up without thinking. It was down there, under that plinth that fell. You can see where it was creased by its weight." Alis pointed to the chunk of metal she'd been threatening Jon with earlier.

Gus kept right on eyeing them. "So you came over to confront Whitfield *before* you knew he'd authorized some kind of sale? Jon?" He added the name like he suspected Jon's story wouldn't match up with Alis's.

With good reason, Jon thought, but at least he had a reasonable answer for this one. "We came over to ask City Hall what the hell was going on. Then we found this mess, and this letter, and—"

"You said you thought he was trying to make a buck," Gus said precisely. "And that *then* you came over and found the mess and thought things were worse than that."

That was, in fact, what Jon had said. He hadn't remembered. No *wonder* it was a bad idea to talk to cops. He stared at Gus until the other man sighed. "I know for a fact that you were at the faire Friday afternoon, so this isn't going to get pinned on you, but for Christ's sake, Jon, either get your story straight or keep your damn mouth shut. This," he said to Alis, with a shake of the carbon paper, "is useful, so thank you, but get out of here, both of you, and do *not* get any more involved in this or I *will* throw you in jail for a few days just for irritating me."

Jon had never been so grateful for an escape in his life. Alis grabbed his hand and they hurried out, got into his truck, and drove three blocks away before either of them so much as *breathed.* Then Jon pulled over and hauled Alis into his arms, mumbling, "I'm sorry. I should have kept my mouth shut."

She exhaled in heavy relief, but then elbowed him. "Yes, you should have! You're not a great liar!"

"I'm really not. Bears are kind of honest creatures. Where did you get that carbon paper?" Jon asked, amazed.

"It *was* stuck to the bottom of the plinth. I put it in my pocket and found it again when I was calling 911. No wonder the bank manager, or whoever it was, called Stuart this weekend. I wouldn't want to take some-body's hastily hand-written note as a legitimate…well, not bill of sale, but whatever that was. Release of lands for sale. Which doesn't even really sound legal anyway."

Jon shook his head in agreement. "No, but the whole 'possession is nine-tenths of the law' thing might be enough to keep a court battle going forever. Like, if whoever it is could even get a semi-legal stake on it, exchange money, something like that. You saved our bacon in there, Alis."

"I kind of did." She slumped against him. "How can it still be this early? I'm exhausted."

"Well, somebody did keep you up really late last night."

"Hah. Yeah, somebody did." She smiled, then stole a kiss before sagging against Jon's chest again. "But it's been a really intense morning. Oh, man, I hope your mayor is okay."

"Me too." Jon closed his eyes. "We have Faire all day. I don't know how I'm going to make it through that without losing my mind. Or falling asleep."

"Keep moving and you won't fall asleep, at least. I wish there were—" Alis broke off suddenly. "Okay, look, I have something to tell *you*, and—" Her phone rang, and she groaned, answering it with, "Not now, Jasmine."

Jon heard her sister say, "Yes, now, sorry," as Alis scooted away, and, out of politeness, turned the engine back on and drove them toward the fairgrounds as Alis muttered, nodded, and finally hung up before returning to Jon's side.

"I am so sorry. Apparently one of the other ladies in waiting is really sick and she's got a real role that somebody needs to play today, and they wanted to know if I could do it."

"No, that's fine." Jon shot her a smile. "Does that mean I need to impress some new lady, or do I still have a shot with Alessandra?"

"Oh, man! I don't know! I'll have to ask! I think it's just that Alessandra's getting a promotion for a day or two and I can stick with her romantic storyline with you, but I'll let you know. I should get your phone number," Alis added, sounding surprised. "I don't have it yet."

"That seems almost impossible." Jon rattled the

number off and she put it in her phone, then called his, which rang from his back pocket as they pulled into the fairgrounds parking lot.

"There, that's me. Now we can communicate. I'm going to be memorizing a scene all morning, though, so if I don't get back to you right away, don't panic."

"I won't," Jon promised, smiled into a kiss, and watched her hop out of the truck and run off toward her RV.

It was only then that he wondered why the Red Court coordinators had called her sister, and not Alis herself.

CHAPTER 17

A TEXT CAME in before Alis was even out of her commoner clothes. From Jon, saying, *why didn't they call you instead of your sister?!?*

She said, "Crap," out loud, and Jasmine, helping lay out her dress, glanced up.

"What?"

"Jon wanted to know why they didn't just call me instead of you. There's actually an answer to that, which is I had the phone set to emergency contacts only, so you were the only person who *could* call, but honestly I'm not even sure he realizes you're here so it's weird if they were calling you back in Maryland or something."

"Also, they didn't call. Or they did, but nobody answered, so somebody came out to the RV and woke me up and told me they needed me on set by a quarter to eleven. I tell you what, I had a really bad moment there before I realized they thought they were talking to you."

Alis couldn't help a laugh. "Honestly, Jazz, I'm going to have to come clean pretty soon here so you stop having to deal with that kind of thing."

"It's the first time it's ever happened. If it happens again, yes, definitely, but in the meantime you can just tell Sword Boy that you had your phone off so you could concentrate on his fabulous abs." Jasmine paused. "They *are* fabulous, right?"

"Oh my *God*, Jazz. You have no *idea*."

"Nope! That's it! That's all I need to hear!" Jasmine lifted her hands like she was putting up a sound barrier. "Glad it all worked out for you, now put your pretty dress on and go be a lady fair. Please tell me I don't have to be Lady Alessandra today? I want to finish this project by tonight."

"No, you're good. I don't fight again until the jousts on Saturday. Although I might go do the informal bouts in the unarmored division sometime this week if I finish playing this bigger part. I don't want a bigger part," Alis mumbled as she squirmed into her dress. "I like being a small fish and the Black Knight."

"Wouldn't it be fun to be a big fish and the Black Knight, though?" Jasmine zipped her up, then returned to her computer. "Lady Alessandra swaggering down out of the stands to strap her armor on while the crowd goes wild? It'd be great."

"Not until I've come out. Which I almost did to Jon, before you called."

"Whoa!" Jasmine's head popped up from behind the computer screen. "Whoa, whoa, what! Two days ago you were like 'no, nay, never!' on that topic! He must be a really good lay!"

"You are totally gross. And he totally is. But even if he wasn't, I just...I kind of really like him, Jazz."

"Well, far be it from me to advise caution, but once that cat's out of the bag it's out for good. A secret known to three people is only a secret if six of them are dead." Jasmine squinted over the screen. "Or something like that."

Alis said, "Yeah," slowly. "It's just that he also told me something kinda big—"

"La la la la la la la I can't heaaaaar you I don't waaaaaant to know about his big things—"

Alis, laughing, gave up and went to Faire.

THE WHOLE RED Court was in a dither when Alis arrived. The Red Queen, Tamira, backstage, fell on her with a hug of relief. "Alis, thank goodness. Princess Cecilia is out—"

"Wait wait what! The princess? That's a huge role!"

Tamira froze. "You said that was okay, though?"

Alis hadn't said any such thing. *Jasmine* had said it was okay. *Jasmine*, who didn't have to *be* Princess Cecilia.

Alis was going to keeeeeel her. Keeeeeel her with knives, or at least a very sharp tongue-lashing. "No, right, sorry, I just thought—I thought I was stepping into a lady-in-waiting position and one of the ladies was stepping up."

"Oh, but no, no." Tamira's huge brown eyes got even bigger. She managed to not quite wince, but got very quiet. "Let's just say they're never going to make a living as actors, okay? But I've seen you at the lists."

Alis's stomach dropped. The Red Queen couldn't possibly have seen through her disguise as the Black Knight. Or could she? Maybe she could have. Or—

"You're great at cheering the knights on and making them all think they're your favorite," Tamira went on. "And I know you can memorize lines. So, please? Is that okay?"

It was amazingly not okay. It was way out of Alis's comfort zone. But she'd kind of already promised, so she found herself nodding. "Yes, of course. I just didn't realize what I was getting myself into. Okay, but—oh, God." She stared at Tamira. "The princess is being courted by somebody from the Silver Court, right? Who? I have this storyline building with the tavern owner, one of the minstrels—"

"Oh, I've seen him," Tamira said admiringly. "The one with the knee brace? Super hot."

"No, the other one. Even hotter. It's a good story-line," or at least a good real-life romance, however brief, "and I don't really want to disrupt it..."

"I'm sure it'll be fine. You shouldn't have to drop that. Shelly should be back tomorrow. I think. I hope. She thinks it's food poisoning but whatever it is, she says she's sick as a dog." Tamira made a face. "It's probably that perfume she's been wearing, though, my God. I guess her sister makes it so she feels obliged, but... Anyway, the poor thing said she tried to come in today because the show must go on, you know? But she said she threw up three times in the car and thought even if she could make it to Faire, people weren't going to want to see a puking princess."

"Yeah, no, she's right about that. And if it's not food poisoning the rest of us don't want to get it."

"Exactly!" Tamira beamed at her. "So hopefully just for today, okay?"

Alis nodded. With any luck Shelly would be fine tomorrow and Alis could pick up Lady Alessandra's storyline and get back to the in-story romance with Jon, but until then, she needed to know: "Okay, but who is it I'm supposed to be flirting with? Cecilia's future husband, I mean? I know I should know, but I haven't been paying that much attention."

"Well, at least that's not going to be a struggle," Tamira said with a knowing smile. "It's Lord Argent, the Silver Knight."

Yup. Alis was going to *murder* her sister.

Tamira obviously saw Alis's face fall, and her own lit up with alarm. "Oh, no, am I wrong? Is it going to be a problem?"

"Gaaaah. No. It'll be fine. He just kind of got on my nerves at the lists the other day." By *cheating.* Alis took a deep breath and shook her head. "It'll be fine. It's just for today."

"Great. Thank you. The other reason I hoped you would do it is that you and Shelly are about the same size, so you can wear her costumes."

Alis squeaked. "Oh, but—" All her costumes had

matches so Jasmine could easily switch places with her. They obviously didn't have any of Shelly's much more elaborate princess gowns copied.

Which was *fine*, Alis told herself. It would only be for today. She didn't fight again for another couple days. "Mine won't do?" she asked anyway, but Tamira laughed.

"Come on, hon. Yours are very pretty, but they're nowhere near fancy enough. Let's get you dressed, and I'll let the Silver Court know you're playing Cecilia today." Tamira sent a text, and got down to the business of helping Alis climb into a genuinely gorgeous red and gold gown with a long corset and full skirt. Unfortunately, Tamira was right and Shelly's perfume really clung to the dress, cloyingly sweet and sickly stinky at the same time. Alis held her breath as somebody settled a glittering rhinestone ruby tiara into her hair, but she couldn't hold her breath all day. Once her hair was dealt with, the hairdresser stepped back and applauded.

"Princess Cecilia is ready for court."

Princess Cecilia, Alis thought, couldn't run or fight in this dress. Or breathe, but that was the perfume, not the dress itself. Well, she wasn't supposed to, anyway. Run or fight, that was. Still, the fact she couldn't annoyed her. Her own dresses were much less cumbersome.

Stop that, she told herself. It would be fine, for one day. It might even be kind of fun.

And it was. The kids were even more enthralled with a 'princess' than they were with Alis's usual lady of the court. She had more fun than she expected taking pictures and discussing the weather, the shopping, and the pretend politics of the courts with both the other members of her court and the general public.

And when Jon came by to say hello, his jaw actually dropped before he swept a low, gallant bow and pretended to be afraid to rise above himself and kiss her hand. He looked rather wonderful himself, with his hair loose but wavy now from its braids, his high-waisted pantaloons and blousy shirt, and the lute he was carrying around strung across his back. Alis, in her best high-falutin' princess voice, said, "Oh, do play for me, minstrel," and Jon bowed again before slinging his lute to the front and striking up a love song.

Queen Tamira drifted by, eyes sparkling even as she looked down her nose at the 'poor' minstrel. "My daughter, you must not lower yourself to consort with the peasants, no matter how sweet their songs might be."

Alis couldn't resist crying, "But Mama, I love him," to the absolute delight of the growing crowd. "My heart could belong to no other!"

"You know you are betrothed to the Silver Knight," Tamira said in severe tones. "Come away, my daughter. Tarry not with these lowlifes."

Several people in the crowd called out protests, and Jon, obviously sensing an opportunity, changed his song to one flattering the wisdom, beauty, and above all, kindness of the queen. Tamira simpered and dimpled, drawn in by his charm, and the crowd applauded as she visibly softened to him. Alis was just about ready to suggest throwing over the whole story-line she was *supposed* to do in favor of the princess running away with the minstrel when a cool, icy voice cut through the music.

"What foul stench is this? A wastrel, tormenting the ears and eyes of my beloved betrothed? Begone, filthy swain, lest I teach you a lesson with my blade." The Silver Knight sauntered up, a titter of appreciation running through the crowd as it parted for him.

If she didn't already know he was a wretched cheat, even Alis would think the man was worth tittering over. He was a fine example of slender masculine beauty, dressed in silver, of course, the fabric very thin and fine and layered, with swooping elfin shoulders and a high collar that made the most of his slender height. Unlike at the lists, his long hair was now loose and very straight, held out of his face by a silver crown. At his side he wore a peace-knotted sword, which meant he couldn't draw it, but he still put his hand on the hilt as he sneered down at Jon.

Jon dropped his gaze and Alis could see the irrita-tion in his smile, for all that he knew this was a perfor-mance and that as an interloper and a peasant, he had a specific part to play. After a moment, he looked up with an expression that was difficult to call a smile at all. "I would hardly recommend you offer that lesson, my lord, as it was my own brother who broke your nose some two seasons past, and he is but a stripling compared to me."

Alis thought, *Uh-oh,* as anger flashed over Lord Argent's face. Tamira, at Alis's side, caught her breath, then caught Alis's wrist in warning. Alis thought, *dammit*, and clapped her hands together, trying to sound light and trilling as she called, "Good my Lord Argent, how splendid to see you. Come, enjoy this minstrel's music with us a while, before the tavern calls him back to his duties."

Argent smiled the smile that made her want to punch him in the teeth and came to her side, slipping his arm through hers. Alis swore her skin actually tried to crawl off her body and run away, even though they were both in long sleeves and not really touching at all. He smelled slightly flat and tangy, not like sweat, but like he was actually made of the silver he was named for. It was surprisingly unpleasant.

Alis cast a slightly desperate look at Jon, who gave another tight smile, rose, and sang an absolutely magnificent song about a lady fair, a wicked knight, and true love found with a poor man. Tamira, at Alis's other side, had to cough twice in order to hide her laughter, and Argent stood beside her positively seething. "What a foolish song," he said when it ended. "Everyone knows that a wise woman chooses security and wealth over love."

"Perhaps in the Silver Court, my lord," Alis said acidly, "but we mortals here in the Red Court enjoy our fierce passions, brief as they may be."

"And yet we are betrothed," Argent said, ice in his tone again. "Perhaps that brief, fierce passion will be mine after all. Your majesty." He bowed to the Red Queen, lifted Alis's hand to kiss the back of it, and walked away, deliberately knocking his shoulder into Jon's.

A cheer went up from the crowd, who were completely delighted with the performance. Jon's jaw locked, however, and Alis saw him barely restrain himself from going after Argent. Then he exhaled, shot Alis herself a wry look, and, in the moment that Tamira looked away, blew her a kiss. The crowd yelped with delight again as relief, laughter, and joy swept through Alis. Somehow she'd been afraid that having to play this stupid part would mess things up between herself and Jon, but he clearly understood how to lean into the whole situation.

Ugh, why did it have to be Argent, though? Alis let Tamira lead her back into the Red Court's tent, where the queen grinned hugely at her. "Did you set that up? That was perfect."

"No! It did play well, though, didn't it," Alis admitted reluctantly.

"Beautifully. If you end up playing Cecilia again tomorrow, we should do this again. The crowd was eating it up with a spoon."

"They were." Alis didn't think the Silver Knight had been, though. She glanced out toward the commoners, then back at Tamira. "Shelly and he don't have a thing going on, do they? In real life, I mean?"

"God, no, I don't think so. Why?"

"I don't know. Argent's just convincingly, one might say creepily, possessive. Is he like that in real life?"

"I don't really know," the queen said with a shrug. "A lot of the Silver Court are from out of town and I don't know the actors very well. I assume he's just good at his job."

"Yeah, I guess. I'll still be happy when Shelly's back."

Tamira gave her a knowing grin. "I bet that minstrel will be too."

Alis smiled and nodded, and as soon as she could, escaped being a princess and went to find Jon.

CHAPTER 18

Jon spent half the afternoon scolding himself for having gotten so in-your-face with Lord Argent, and his bear spent the same amount of time going, *But we could have swatted him! We could have knocked him right into the trees! We could have eaten his face!* until Jon finally gave up yelling at himself so he could laugh at the bear.

I know, buddy. It's just that for one, this is a performance, and for two, I'm pretty sure Alis can take care of a creep like that on her own.

*But your brother **did** break his pointy nose,* the bear said with tremendous satisfaction.

Jon grinned. "Yes, he did. And I wouldn't have hated doing it again myself, but that wouldn't be chivalric."

The bear snorted dismissively. *Chivalry is for humans.*

"Which I am most of the time!"

No, his bear said. *You are a shifter who lives in human form most of the time. That isn't quite the same.*

That seemed insightful enough that Jon decided

he'd better stop talking to the bear, particularly out loud, and instead consider what it had to say. He was back at the tavern, alternating between playing with the minstrel group and serving beers, while Laurie lurched around on a leg that was fully healed but still had to be braced. *That*, of all things, was what made Jon decide the bear was right. Shifters might live most of their lives as humans, and might be very human in most ways, but they really weren't quite the same. It was an interesting thought. Probably not one that mattered very much, but interesting just the same.

The last set piece of the day for the Court actors was at five. Jon pretended he wasn't waiting anxiously for Alis to come by the tavern after that, mostly by running himself ragged serving drinks and bantering in Ye Olde English with patrons. Although it turned out one of the patrons was an actual medievalist, and pointed out that *Old* English was nearly a different language from modern English, and that their mock-Shakespearian was just playing with early modern English.

Then the guy looked into his drink, sighed, and said, "I'm a lot of fun at parties," which made the girl next to him laugh out loud. The next thing Jon knew the two of them were walking off together, chatting happily. He was still trying to decide if that had been a very clever pickup line on the guy's part, or if the dude had just gotten really lucky, when Alis arrived.

She was in a denim skirt and green bandeau shirt, her thick curling hair bouncing around her shoulders, and looking about as far from the Red Princess as she could get. Jon saw her first, watched her searching the busy tavern for him, and got to see her face light up when she found him in the crowd. She glanced down, and a minute later his phone buzzed. He balanced a drinks tray, checked the phone, smiled, and nodded toward her: the message had said, *I'll hang out until you can get away.*

Alis gave him a thumbs up and retreated to the edge of the tavern's property, perching on a tree-stump seat there, and Jon went back to work with a vengeance. If he could get everybody's drinks to them fast enough, they'd go home sooner, right?

You should feed them apples, his bear suggested. *Autumn apples that make them dizzy.*

That's kind of what beer is, he told the animal cheerfully. *Some of these are even actually apple cider.*

We should have some apple cider!

The idea was tempting, but there were too many puzzles to solve. Having a dizzy head wouldn't help. *Maybe later,* he promised the bear, which agreed happily. Lucky for Jon, bears didn't have a great sense of time: 'later' could mean never, and it wouldn't think anything of it.

It was a solid half hour before the crowd started to thin. One of the other tavern swains waved him away, and Jon went to grab a couple of Thunder Bear root beers for himself and Alis, only to discover, when he got to her, that his wretched brother was already there with root beers. Worse, Alis was laughing, and laughed harder when Jon arrived, although she did tilt her chin up for a smiling kiss. "Believe it or not," she said preemptively, "he's not telling stories on you. He was telling me about how he broke Argent's nose a couple years ago. God, I wish I'd seen that."

"The bastard cheated," Laurie said. "Flashed something in my eyes. I wanted to get him down so I could see what it was, but I still don't know, so I couldn't go to the faire committee to complain."

"He did that t—!" Alis broke off and took a huge swallow of root beer that ended up sending her into a coughing fit. Both the brothers stared at her in consternation as she waved her hands, evidently indicating she was okay, and finally, with tears streaming down her face and possibly some root beer streaming from her nose, she said, "He *did* that to you?" hoarsely.

Jon, worriedly, said, "Are you okay?" and she nodded, wiping root beer off her nose.

"Yeah, I just, uh, don't like cheaters. It's really good root beer." She scrunched her whole face, nose wrinkled, mouth pinched, eyes closed, before she stretched it all the opposite way and added, "Although not so great through the nose. Ow."

"Here." Jon handed her one of the root beers he'd brought over. "This one doesn't have cough and tears and snot all over it."

Alis burst out laughing and carefully traded the drinks. "Neither did Laurie's before I lost control of my face. There's got to be some way to get proof. I'm fi… aah, I'm fine. Somebody must be filming those fights. From the right angle a camera could catch it."

"Dozens of people film them, but we can't go around absconding with everybody's phone to check their footage," Laurie said. "You go to all of them, right? As a courtier? Maybe you can get the other ladies and court members to record them—"

"With phones we're not supposed to have in character?"

"Oh, dammit. Right. Well, Jon, you're fighting him tomorrow in the unarmored division, right? Maybe we can strap a camera to your helmet." Laurie looked up toward the sky thoughtfully. "Actually, that's a great idea. I bet I could build a whole streaming audience empire off first-person-point-of-view fights."

"Not off my first person point of view!"

"You're no fun," Laurie told him.

Alis mumbled, "I disagree," and Laurie managed to look both horrified, shocked, and gleeful all at the same time. He opened his mouth to say something, and whatever it was, Jon didn't want to hear it, so he stuck his finger in Laurie's mouth.

His brother made a series of garbled sounds that ended in a hacking cough, knocking Jon's hand away, and an incredibly injured expression. "I wasn't going to say *anything*!"

"And I made sure of it." Jon smiled as placidly as he could and Laurie hunched up in a sulk.

"Fine. I'm going back to the tavern, where they *appreciate* me."

"You do that." Jon took a long, languid sip of his own root beer as Laurie sulked off, and Alis laughed.

"You two are pretty close, huh?"

"Yeah. We annoy each other all the time, but yeah,

Laurie's got my back. You think Lord Argent's really cheating?"

"I'm sure of it," Alis said, unexpectedly decisively. "But I don't know how to prove it either. The helmet camera is kind of a great idea, but anyway, never mind him. Did you hear anything about what happened to the mayor?"

"Only the gossip that's going around, which is that he wasn't home, either. I don't know. I feel like I should go look for him, which is stupid. It's not like I can track him in the only way I'd be any good at it." A smile pulled at the corner of his mouth at the idea, though, and he dropped his voice. "But that would be pretty great, wouldn't it? All the shifters in town out there sniffing around in their animal forms? It would look like the circus got loose, or something."

"It would look like the second half of Jurassic Park," Alis said with a laugh. "All the running and the screaming from the normies."

Jon winced all the way through his entire soul. "True humans. That's what we call you."

"That's more flattering, but less funny." Alis scooted closer, until her body heat mingled with Jon's, and lowered her voice even more. "Would it work? If you were all able to go sniffing around?"

"I don't know," Jon admitted softly. "It sure looked like a shifter had been at City Hall, but there wasn't any scent of one at all."

"Do shifters…" Alis paused, clearly trying to work through the question, then shook her head. "No, you're just going to have to explain it all to me. Do you have better senses of smell when you're in human form than we do? Do shifters *smell* different? Do shifter *animals* smell different from…true bears, or whatever?"

Jon seized on the first question, because it was the only one he knew a concrete answer to: "Yes, we smell better than true hu—"

Alis, to his horror, leaned in and took a good solid whiff of his armpit, then leaned back again with a delicately offended expression. "I don't think you smell better at all."

Jon curdled red from somewhere beneath his lungs all the way to the top of his scalp. Alis threw her head back and roared with laughter, tears leaking from her eyes, and when she'd about stopped, she looked at Jon's mortified hunch and dissolved into laughter again. "I'm sorry, I'm sorry, you smell *fine*, I just couldn't resist. I didn't ask if you *smelled* better, I asked if you had better *senses* of smell—" She broke down into laughter again, the giggles so infectious that Jon couldn't help ducking his head and smiling too.

By that time they'd drawn attention, and it was clear that some of the minstrel band were planning to come join them. Jon, still blushing, tilted his head away from the crowd. "I think if we're going to talk about who smells better we should do it somewhere else."

"So they don't all know?" Alis slugged the rest of her root beer back, opened her mouth to say something else, and let out a belch that silenced everybody in a twenty-foot radius. Then *she* blushed as furiously as Jon had as a round of applause went up and people started calling "Ten out of ten, top score!", "No, it lacked resonance, eight out of ten," and, "Extra points for style!"

"I think getting out of here is a good idea," Alis said through her blush, and Jon, grinning, got up, offered her a hand, and drew her away into a quieter part of the faire. The attendees were heading out now: the gates closed at six during the week, and everybody who didn't work there had to be off the grounds by seven at the latest. It was nearly that now. Once they'd gotten away from the tavern, Alis repeated, "So they *don't* all know?", then looked up at Jon with a winsome expression he thought would cut his heart right in two. "Sorry if I'm asking too many questions. This is all pretty incredible and I hardly know what I don't know to ask about."

You should tell her about mates, his bear told him in no uncertain terms.

I will, Jon promised. *I just...I really want to meet the Black Knight, first. I want to...* He sighed internally. *I want to understand what draws me to him. I've never **had** a boyfriend. I've never really even thought about having a boyfriend!*

Mates are mates, the bear said. *You worry too much about it all.*

Well, that's humans for you, Jon said, then shook his head at Alis, knowing the conversation with the bear had taken essentially no time in the outside world. "No, it's okay to ask all the questions you want. I want you to. It's just that some of them I might not have ever had to think about an answer to."

"Like who smells better," Alis said, her eyes sparkling, and he laughed.

"Yeah, exactly. Let me try that one again: shifters *do* scent better than true humans. Not nearly as well as we do in our animal forms, but better than humans. Cat shifters see really well in the dark. Some of the bird shifters have—well—eagle eyesight. We tend to be stronger than usual, and we almost all hear well."

"So you're saying you're all Wolverine."

Jon made fists like he hoped claws would pop out. "Kind of. Well, yeah, even more than you're thinking, kind of, because shifting helps us heal up. Laurie's knee is actually fine now because he went home and shifted a couple times, but since half the faire crew saw him blow it out, he's stuck in that knee brace for at least as long as it would take for a fast-healing true human to heal."

"I knew somebody in college who smeared himself all over the highway in a motorcycle wreck and they thought he'd be in traction for months. He was out in a few weeks. Like that?"

"Yeah, but don't tell Laurie about that or he'll try tell everybody he healed up overnight. Low profile," Jon said wryly. "We try to keep a low profile, generally speaking."

"So no famous shifters?" Alis asked.

"Well. No, actually, there are some really famous shifters, but medically speaking, I mean."

Alis's eyes rounded. "Who? No, you're probably not supposed to tell me. But now I'm going to be looking at every celebrity and trying to suss out if they're secretly an octopus or something." She paused. "Are there octopus shifters?"

"I…have never met one. That doesn't mean no, but…" Jon blinked down at her, and Alis grinned.

"Okay, look, let's go back to the basics. Scents. *Do* shifters smell different from true bears or whatever?"

"You know, I haven't really spent a lot of time sniffing wild animals—"

Alis burst into laughter again and this time Jon couldn't help joining her. "This is not a conversation I was prepared to have!"

"I guess not! But okay, fair, it makes sense that you probably don't know that much about what true bears smell like. Do you smell different from true humans?"

"It's not really a scent," Jon said slowly. "We can generally recognize each other, but it's kind of more a…*knowing*…than a scent or a way somebody moves. But the City Hall didn't smell like any kind of shifter had been there, and I would definitely have been able to smell bear or cat or…" He shrugged, unable to think of anything else with claws that big.

"Gryphons?" Alis asked hopefully. "Dragons?"

"Only in legend, as far as I know. What," he said at her disappointed *hmph*, "aren't bear shapeshifters enough for you?"

"Well. When you put it that way, I guess so. It's pretty magical, for sure. All right, so." She ducked into a copse of pine trees, patted a mossy heap, and settled down on it, inhaling the warm sweet-scented air. "So what we know is that for some reason Mayor Whitfield wrote a letter initiating the process of selling the fairgrounds, which was delivered to the bank late Friday afternoon. Handwritten, which is hinky, and on carbon paper, which is nuts but also suggests he wanted to leave a record, right? How old is this guy?" she added. "Like, who would think of using carbon paper? Who would have it lying around?"

"He's in his sixties," Jon said. "And I don't know, but let's be glad he did. You're right. I didn't think of it in terms of him intending to leave a record. That kind of suggests he thought he was in trouble, doesn't it?"

"I think so." Alis leaned against Jon, distractingly warm and soft. "But unless he's a shifter, he couldn't have put up that much of a fight, could he? City Hall was wrecked and you just said even in their human forms shifters are stronger than true humans. And whether he is or not, there was visual evidence of a shifter but no lingering scent. Hm."

"Are you secretly Miss Marple?" Jon asked, impressed.

"Hah! No, I have a totally different secret identity. Two of them, in a way," Alis said, obviously amused at herself. "In fact—"

"Lady Alessandra vs Princess Cecilia," Jon intoned. "A fight to the death! Only the winner will be allowed to resume her life as Alis Carbuncle."

"Capellas!"

Jon ducked his head toward hers, shoulders shaking with quiet laughter. "I knew it wasn't Carbuncle, but I'd only heard you say it once and couldn't remember quite what it was. Capellas is nicer than Carbuncle."

"Oh, you think? Do you know what a carbuncle *is*?"

Jon screwed up his face. "I'm afraid I do."

"They're disgusting! Are you saying I'm disgusting?"

Jon went for that kiss he'd been planning on, nudging Alis backward into the moss. "Gross is the farthest thing from my mind when I think of you, my lady fair."

"Unh. Good answer," Alis breathed as the kiss ended. "But if we're doing this out here, you get to be on bottom. I don't want twigs poking me in the ass."

Jon levered up on an elbow, trying to look hurt. "But you don't mind *me* getting twig-poked?"

"You *just* told me you can shift and heal from most injuries."

"Oh. Yeah. Fair," Jon murmured, and was obligingly the bottom.

CHAPTER 19

IF SOMEONE HAD TOLD Alis she would spend a night in the woods, sleeping in moss, and wake up warm and comfortable, she would simply not have believed it. There was a *reason* she and Jasmine had the RV, and it wasn't just that Jazz needed electricity to do her job. Alis was firmly in the 'glamping' faction of campers: she wanted hot water, toilets, and mattresses.

Or, it appeared, she wanted Jon Torben, who was none of those things, but made a bed of moss the coziest place in the whole world to sleep. He'd tucked around her, radiating heat, and she'd slept undisturbed until sunlight started seeping through the trees. Alis briefly contemplated just staying there forever, though in the end, the idea made her snicker. She bet Jon would be just as warm and cozy curled up sleeping as a bear in four feet of snow, but she doubted he could keep her warm enough to hibernate through the winter. Maybe just a summer fling, then.

Except the idea made her heart hurt. A summer

didn't sound like enough time to spend with him. A week *certainly* wasn't. A lifetime sounded like it might be a good start.

Which was really not the kind of thing she was accustomed to thinking. She wasn't anti-relationship, or anything. She just had a life of her own and hadn't met anybody yet who was worth disrupting that for.

Or maybe more accurately, she had never *previously* met anybody worth disrupting it for. But that would be a hell of a thing to say to a guy she'd known for five days. "Enjoy it while you can," she told herself aloud, if quietly, but Jon stirred behind her, and tucked her closer, mumbling, "Morning," into her hair.

"Kind of a perfect one," she murmured back, and felt him smile against her shoulder as he nestled her even more solidly against him. It was immediately evident *that* kind of behavior was going to keep them in the moss a good while longer this morning.

It was too early to go solve a mystery anyway. Alis slid her hand backward between their bodies and curled her fingers around Jon's cock, waking him all the way up with a, "Jesus Christ, yes, *God*," that turned a perfect morning into an even better one. They were still up and leaving the fairgrounds long before most employees were starting to arrive, and if they were both wearing yesterday's rumpled clothes, nobody in Renaissance batted an eye to have a man in a tunic and pirate pants and a woman in a kirtled dress show up for coffee and croissants at a local cafe.

"I had a thought," Alis said over the coffee. They'd taken a table outside, as far away from the other morning customers as they could. Jon lifted sleepy brown eyes to her, the sunlight brightening them to almost gold, and she had a lot of other thoughts, none of which were about the topic she'd meant to bring up. She ended up smiling foolishly at him. "Has anybody ever told you how incredibly handsome you are?"

"My mom, but I think she may be biased."

"Well, I'm not, and you are. You should be, I don't know. Modeling for a fireman's calendar, or something."

Jon laughed quietly and brought his coffee up to his face, mostly to inhale its scent, as far as she could tell. "I'm not a fireman."

"I hate to break it to you, man, but neither are most of those models." At his expression of genuine surprise, she giggled. "You didn't really think every firehouse in the country had a dozen impossibly hot, stacked men waiting around for their close-up, did you?"

"I kinda did!"

"Okay, well, let's pretend I haven't broken your illusions and go back to my thought that was *not* about hot men."

"If we have to." He smiled over the coffee, which he still seemed to be intent on inhaling rather than drinking.

"I was thinking we could go out to the mayor's house and see if you could pick up a scent there. Just in case."

Jon regarded her thoughtfully. "Gus is a shifter, too, you know. The police officer from City Hall that we talked to."

"Implying he could have gone and sniffed around, but were the other people with him shifters, or would he have been constrained by having to pretend to be human while they searched? Also, he sent other people to the mayor's house, he didn't go himself."

"You *are* Miss Marple."

"I'm much hotter than Miss Marple." Alis made a face. "At least, I hope I am. Can't I be, I don't know, Enola Holmes or something? Miss Fisher, maybe? Although Enola's too young," she muttered to herself. "And with Miss Fisher it depends on whether you go with the age the character is in the books, or the age of the actress who played her. The book character's the right age but honestly it made way more sense for her to be the age the actress was."

Jon blinked at her slowly over the coffee cup and Alis glared half-heartedly in return. "I take it you don't actually watch many murder mystery shows. Or read them."

"I'm afraid my murder mystery repertoire is limited to Miss Marple, Jessica Fletcher, and Sherlock Holmes. Oh, and Hercule Poirot, but I think having two Agatha Christie characters in there is cheating, or something. Who's Enola?" he asked, sounding legitimately fascinated.

"Sherlock's non-canonical younger sister, from a modern young adult series that was made into a series of television movies. They're kind of great, actually," Alis said, distracted. "Both the books and the movies. A lot of fun. Oh, and you should read the Murder Most Unladylike series, they're wonderful. And—"

Jon was grinning now. A huge happy cat-in-the-sunshine kind of smile. Or bear in the sunshine, Alis guessed. "How do you know all this?"

"I teach third grade!"

"And memorize murder mysteries! You *will* solve this whole mess!"

"Only if it's structured like an Arthur Conan Doyle book," Alis said wryly. "Anyway, yes, no? Is it a good idea or a bad one? Sniffing around, I mean."

"Oh! Good one. Although if he's got neighbors, or if the cops are there to keep an eye on the place, a bear sniffing around is not subtle. It'd help if I was a raccoon or something."

Alis couldn't help a laugh. "Raccoons are not nearly as sexy as bears. Stick with what works."

"See, why is that? Why are bears sexy and raccoons aren't? Why does that matter? Isn't being a shifter the sexy part?" They finished their coffee and croissants, which weren't nearly as good as yesterday's cinnamon rolls, and threw the remains away before heading for the truck.

"I have no answer for that," Alis admitted. "I guess it's that bears are big dangerous predators and we live in a society that tells us big dangerous men are hot?"

"*I'm* not dangerous!"

Alis eyed him and Jon looked a bit abashed as they drove through town. "All right, I guess I could be. But I'm not one of those assholes who goes around snarling and pushing people around and treating women like crap, which seems to be a big part of the whole sexy dangerous guy thing."

"Did I mention society is broken? No, it's the Beauty and the Beast thing, the 'I can make him better,' although let me point out that Beauty does not make the Beast better. He does that himself, even in the earliest versions of the story. He wants to be worthy of her, so he works on himself. That's the only way people change, is if they want to."

"I feel I've stepped into a hot button topic."

Alis smirked. "I could go on about this one for hours, but I'll spare you."

"Don't," Jon said with what sounded like honest enthusiasm. "I'd really love to hear it. I like hearing what you think."

Alis accidentally said, "Oh yeah, he's a keeper," out loud, and Jon beamed.

"I'm glad to hear it. We'll figure out the details later."

"Hah! Okay!" The funny thing was, Alis kind of thought Jon might mean it, although as they were apparently pulling up to the mayor's house, this wasn't the time to dive into that.

There was, in fact, a cop lingering in front of a longish driveway: a bluntly built woman pacing back and forth. The house itself was set back into the woods, almost on the mountain, and had no immediate neighbors, although there were houses on either side of the large lot. The cop waved as Jon and Alis climbed out of the truck, and Jon shook her hand. "Hey, Fran. This is Alis, she's with the Faire. She and I found—"

"Yeah, you were in City Hall yesterday morning." Fran was broad-shouldered and broad-hipped, with a reserved smile and heavy eyebrows. "What can I do for you, Jon?"

"I was hoping I could sniff around," Jon said so forthrightly that Alis suddenly suspected Fran was a shifter, too. Fran lifted an eyebrow in Alis's direction and Jon nodded. "She knows."

Fran exhaled explosively. "Well, I'm paired up with Sully. He went to get coffee, so you've got a minute, but he *doesn't* know, so be careful. I had a sniff around myself. Nothing." She paused, shook her head, and repeated, "Nothing. Maybe you'll catch something I didn't."

"Is it—can I—is it rude to ask?" Alis asked both nervously and hopefully.

Fran gave her a semi-quelling look. "Yeah, kind of, but I'm a badger. More subtle than a grizzly," she said to Jon, pointedly, "but not a lot of them around here so I had to be quick myself. Go, before Sully gets back with the coffee. I've already been walking around out here like an idiot for twenty minutes."

"Where'd he go, Denver? Be back in a minute." Jon hurried down the driveway, disappearing behind the house before he shifted. Alis stood frozen, not sure if she should follow him or stay with Fran, but it wasn't like she spoke bear, so anything Jon learned would require him becoming human again anyway.

Fran folded her arms and looked Alis up and down without saying anything. Alis had no idea if she passed muster or not, and offered a careful smile. "Sorry for being rude. I'm new to all this."

The officer's heavy eyebrows rose. "Oh really. How new?"

"Like, yesterday new?"

A little to her surprise, Fran's expression softened a bit. "Oh, *new* new. Jon told you? Out of the blue?"

"Kind of? He wanted to see if the claw marks on the reception counter at City Hall were shifter-sized and he couldn't do that without telling me."

"Uh-*huh*." For some reason, the officer sounded amused. "Sure. That's a reason."

Well, it was. Alis, slightly offended, frowned at the other woman. "Do you think he's okay? The mayor, I mean. Not Sully. Or Jon." She glanced toward the house, where presumably Jon was just fine. It was a nice house, smaller than she expected for a mayoral residence, but she didn't think it was an official residence, just where he lived.

Whatever had amused Fran disappeared and she shook her head. "I hope so. This sounds cliched, but this kind of thing doesn't happen in Renaissance. Chester is a good guy. I hope nothing's happened to him."

"If you got what you wanted out of him, why would you also take him? Or—" Alis shivered. "Or worse."

"I suppose so he couldn't go back on the deal he'd made. None of it's going to hold up in court as it is. The council would have to sign off on a deal to sell the land, for one thing, and they haven't, but besides that, it's pretty clear he was coerced into signing what he did, and since the bank slowed everything down even before Mackenzie Torben put in an injunction stopping the sale, it's not even likely whoever is behind this is gonna end up with possession of the land being on their side."

"Then why would they do it?" Alis rubbed her face. "What good is a few days of disruption?"

"Well, you gotta assume they figured they were going to get away with it. It's a messy damn way to do business, though. Makes me think it's some kind of personal beef, not a corporate move. That'd be tidier. The bank's forensic accountants are following the account trail. They'll come up with a name."

"Even if it's hidden behind shell corporations?" Alis waved a hand, a little embarrassed. "All I know about that kind of thing is from television and movies. Don't they end up in a lot of dead ends?"

Fran offered her half a grin. "Mostly only in the movies. You gotta be dealing with *real* money to bury an account through so many shells that the owner can't be found, but most people figure, they get away with it in the movies, so I probably can now. It's also not as fast as it is in the movies." She glanced toward the house, obviously wishing Jon would hurry it up. "It goes faster if there's a dead body to link to it, because then there are murder charges and that can loosen some red tape, but we'd all rather it didn't end up that way."

"God. Yeah. Thank you." Alis gave the officer a shy smile. "I didn't know any of that, and I know you didn't have to tell me any of it, so thanks."

"Well, anything for Jon's…friend. He's a good guy. There he is. About time."

Alis glanced toward the street, first, wondering if it was Sully returning or Jon who was 'about time,' but luckily, she thought, it was Jon. He came jogging around the house, an interested frown on his features, and shook his head as he approached. "It's just like City Hall. I can scent you, Fran, but otherwise nothing."

"But kind of aggressively nothing, yeah?" Fran was suddenly on point, her dark eyes glittering. "Like *weird* amounts of nothing?"

"Yeah. I don't get it. It's like somebody ran hand sanitizer over everything, except it doesn't have that kind of smell, either. It's just…empty."

Fran nodded. "Yeah. I got Gus to come sniff it out, too, and he didn't pick up anything either."

Alis said, "Oh. That's why you let him do this, isn't it? You thought it was too…neutral? You were hoping he might figure out why?" She felt as if, like the shifters, she might be on the verge of understanding something, but she didn't know *what*.

"Pretty much. I didn't like it, but unless I can pin down what's wrong, it doesn't matter." Fran lifted her chin toward Jon's truck. "So get out of here now, will you? I'd rather not explain to Sully why a Torben was hanging out at my crime scene."

Jon offered her a hand to shake again. "Yeah, will do. Thanks, Fran. I'll let you know if I figure out what the nothing is."

"Yeah, ditto. Nice to meet you, Alis."

"You too." Alis followed Jon back to the truck, both of them deep in thought.

CHAPTER 20

"I DON'T KNOW how amateur sleuths do it," Jon said as they headed back into town. "I feel like I need a true crime podcaster on our side right now, or something. There's got to be a shifter involved, or somebody who knows about us, but honestly, how would you make that kind of mark in the reception desk if you weren't actually a shifter?"

Alis, across the truck bench from him, curved her hand into claws and swiped at the air like she could come up with an answer. "You'd need something either really heavy and incredibly sharp, or heavy and a lot of time. And it sure doesn't look like there was time involved at City Hall. Officer Fran said she thought this was personal, though. Whoever's behind trying to buy the fairgrounds, and everything. She said a corporation would be tidier. No weird handwritten receipts."

Not that it was a receipt, but Jon knew what she meant. "I swear that makes even less sense. Well. It does and doesn't. The idea of some kind of corporate hit man out there threatening and kidnapping a small-town mayor is ludicrous, but if somebody's not trying to buy up the land to put the faire out of business, what the hell's their motivation? I'm sticking with brewery business after this," he added firmly. "Solving mysteries isn't my strong suit."

"Speaking of which, um." Alis cleared her throat. "What's your schedule this summer? You said you and Laurie go around to some of the other faires…?"

A thrill of hope knocked everything mysterious out of Jon's mind. "Yeah, we started expanding East a couple of years ago. It used to be we stuck to the Mountain region, and then we moved out to the Pacific Northwest and California, but we've got our share of the market pretty well solidified in that part of the country, now. I'm scheduled for Kansas, Delaware, and Rhode Island later in the year." He thought his heart might leap out of his chest as he tried very hard to say, "You?" casually, and totally failed.

Alis *heh*ed and looked out the window, smiling nervously. "Ironically I'm going to Seattle and Sacramento over the rest of the summer, so we're not crossing paths at all. But if you'll be around, I mean available, over any of the weekends when you're in Delaware or Rhode Island, I could probably come see you. If you wanted."

She was doing about as good a job as he was at sounding casual. Jon reached for her hand as he idled the truck at a stoplight, and when she looked at him, smiled. "I would love that. I'll make sure to have free time, even if it means dragging Laurie out of the lists by his ear."

Alis gave a little rushing laugh that sounded of relief. "Okay, but I want to see that. I just, um. Well. I'd like to see you again when this week is over."

"Me too. Enough that I'm afraid I'll come across as way too intense and scare you off." The confession rushed out of him like Alis's laugh had, even as his bear more or less rolled its eyes with exasperation.

*She's your **mate**, it said. You **can't** scare her off.*

Yeah, well, I still haven't tried to bring up the whole polyamory problem, so I think being worried she might nope on out of the whole thing is pretty legit.

Although he was sure the bear understood the general idea of what he'd just said, because his emotional state would convey it if nothing else, the animal still gave him a look that indicated Jon's phrasing was incomprehensible. Jon muttered, *I think I have good reason to be worried,* and the bear clearly gave up on him as a hopeless cause.

Alis, in the meantime, gave him another shy smile. "So far I like your intensity. All of it." The way her voice dropped suggested she had some specific things in mind that she liked. Jon seriously considered bailing on the faire entirely so he could bring her home and explore those things. "So Delaware in…what, September? I don't remember when their big faire is."

"Labor Day weekend is when we set up there, but we're there for the whole three weeks."

"Oh, school's out that weekend. I can definitely see

you then. Okay. Whew." She actually said 'whew,' and Jon found himself beaming at her.

"Whew. Yeah. Okay," he added, hoping to alleviate both his own nervousness and hers, "now that we've got our futures set up..."

Alis laughed. "Slow down, cowboy. I don't know that a date ten weeks from now counts as setting our *whole* future up."

"Hey, you're the one bringing our *whole* futures into it! Because I'm not wrong, am I? A date ten weeks from now *is* setting up our future."

Alis popped her mouth closed. "You know, as a school teacher, I tell kids all the time to think about what they want to say before they say it. Maybe I should take my own advice."

"Or not." Jon liked the idea of it being at least the start of their *whole* future, but also still didn't want to make things too intense, despite Alis's apparent approval of intensity. Not until he'd talked to Lord Edward, at least. "Anyway, I was going to say, we've got to get through the shows at the faire today before we can do anything else. I thought I might ask some of the other shifters if they'd ever tried hiding their scents, though. Maybe somebody's got an idea, because I can't figure out how else those claw marks showed up. That's hardwood! *Old* hardwood! It's like iron!"

"I get the impression from what you were saying that it also wiped out most normal human scents, too?" At Jon's nod, Alis went on. "So even if it's not a shifter, it's somebody who knows enough to wipe out scents anyway."

"And can cut through old hardwood."

"And has some kind of vendetta against the fair-grounds." Alis paused a moment. "Is your life always weird like this?"

"Never," Jon said, honestly. "Is yours?"

"Not at all!"

"Do you think we create a weirdness vortex together?"

"God," Alis said with feeling, "I hope not. 'Hi, Mom, Dad. This is Jon, together we make weird.'"

"Oooh. Are you introducing me to the family, then?"

"You introduced me to yours already!"

Jon startled enough that his bear looked up, wondering what it had missed. "I did, didn't I? Would it help if I said I hadn't thought of it like that? Maybe because my parents weren't there?"

"I'm not sure. But in your defense, I don't think you were *introducing me to your family*." She paused again. "More like throwing me into the deep end."

"Hey!"

Alis grinned. "No, I don't mean that. You're just all obviously involved in the faire and Renaissance's businesses in a bunch of different ways, so getting them caught up on what was going on made sense. I didn't think about it as being introduced to the family, either, not until my sister said it. Did your real estate uncle come up with anything, by the way?"

"Uncle Dave? Just that there was no previous interest in the fairgrounds land. No big corporations sniffing around or anything." They pulled into the fair parking lot as he spoke, and Jon leaned over to steal a kiss. "I guess that makes personal motivation more likely, too. Should I come play the lute for you again this afternoon?"

"If Shelly isn't back to play the princess, then God, yes, please. Anything to keep Lord Argent from smarming on me!"

~

LORD ARGENT SMARMED ANYWAY.

He smarmed in the same way the scene had played out yesterday, which—Jon had to admit—was good, because it meant the audience from day to day was getting similar performances, so they would have reference points they could share outside of the faire. Jon didn't *like* Argent. That didn't mean the guy was bad at his job, unfortunately.

And honestly, if Jon was being absolutely fair, most of the reason he didn't like Argent was that *he* wanted to be wooing Alis, instead of letting the lord of the Silver Court do it. It didn't matter if it was all a performance. He was still grumpy about it.

Because that was very mature and professional of him. Jon had to laugh at himself as he headed back from the Red Court to the tavern after their little tete-a-tete. Hopefully Shelly would be feeling better soon and could release Alis from the bother of having to flirt politely with Argent. Then he and Alis could get Armsman Jonathan and Lady Alessandra's romance back on track.

It hit him, as he approached the tavern, that every

time he'd seen Alis in the past few days, that his heart, soul, and bear had called out that she was his mate. The hot and cold thing seemed to have faded. Of course, he hadn't seen Lord Edward in days, because the Black Knight notoriously only showed up for the fights, but that was a problem for later. Jon would find *some* way to talk to the swordsman, and learn where the unexpected twist in his fate was leading him.

Laurie, still hobbling around in his knee brace, waved a greeting to Jon as he arrived, and called, "Good my minstrel, play us a song or two, will you not? Our patrons are calling for a dance!"

This generally meant it wasn't too busy, and sometimes actually got people to dance. Jon sat down, strummed a few bars, then dipped into an instrumental version of a pop song. At first no one noticed, but then a few people turned to listen with confused expressions before realizing what they were hearing. A minute later a bunch of young women who were the song's original target audience were on their feet, dancing together, and broke into cheers and applause when Jon finished.

He bowed where he sat and struck up another tune from a popular tv show that got laughter and coins tossed into the tip jar as they left, singing the chorus to the song at the top of their lungs. Jon was willing to bet half the people at the faire would be singing it before they left tonight, it was that catchy.

"Ah, yes." Lord Argent's disdainful, snotty voice cut through the music. "The minstrel, begging for his coin. How common."

We could swat him, Jon's bear muttered. It was better than the first thought that had leaped to Jon's mind, which was that he could bash the guy with his lute. That would be really hard on the lute, though, so he smiled through his teeth at the silver lord. "If you've another song you'd like to hear, my lord, toss a coin to the minstrel and we'll see what we can do."

"The only tune I wish to hear is the agony of your defeat."

Jon, very obligingly, he thought, switched to a song called *Agony,* which got a laugh from the musical theatre lovers at the tavern, and a sour look from Argent himself. Before he could say anything else, Laurie sauntered up to him. "Will yer high and mightiness be drinking at our humble establishment this evening?"

There was a familiar, craven, whining sort of tone to Laurie's voice. Argent turned to him, his rather fine, handsome features blackening with anger. "*You.*"

"Me, yer lordship. Me and no other. Surely yer high and mightiness honors us with yer graceful presence here. What might we bring for ye, yer lordship?"

"I want nothing from you peasants." Argent curled his lip, and Laurie practically bent double with deference.

"Av carse not, yer mightiness, yer most handsome and regal lordliness, after all, what could a poor auld barman like meself offer a great man like you, yer—"

Jon fumbled a chord as he finally placed his brother's mimicry and fought down a laugh. He switched songs again, to a tune everybody knew if they'd grown up watching a certain Robin Hood movie, and got the words, "Every town," out before half the tavern patrons joined him in the rest of the line.

Argent squinted, then flushed suddenly as he *also* realized what character Laurie was playing, and how that made him the pompous, self-centered villain of the piece. "How *dare* you peasants mock a lord!"

"You make it so easy, yer lordship," Laurie said through a cackling grin, and to Jon's delight, the commoners started to boo and hiss at Argent. He even recognized some lines straight out of the movie.

Argent, turning so red that even his fake elf ears seemed to glow with it, hissed, "They all ended up in jail, you know! In the stocks, and in jail!"

"And Robin broke them out!" somebody yelled. "Away, ya scurrrrvy wolf!"

Lord Argent actually turned and fled to roars of approval and applause. Four people bought Jon a drink. Fortunately, as the evening was starting to wind down, a number of other musicians showed up to help him drink them.

And so did Alis, in a short green dress and laughing as she came to give Jon a kiss. "I'm hearing Lord Argent lost a battle of wits here tonight. That's probably the sexiest thing a guy has ever done."

"Yeah?" Jon beamed at her. "Sexier than Tom Holland's Lip Sync Battle?"

"The second sexiest thing a man has ever done," Alis said without missing a beat.

Jon deflated, but laughed. "I walked right into that, didn't I?"

"You obviously did. Look, I'm absolutely starving but can't face another turkey leg. Want to bring me out for pizza in town?"

"I was just thinking that's what I wanted to do with my evening. Laurie!" Jon waved his brother down. "You okay to close up here?"

"Yeah, but dude, you're gonna owe me when I find my ma—uh, my, uh."

"Management skills?" Jon suggested.

Mate, his bear said. *He was going to say **mate**.*

Yes, I know that, Jon replied, amused.

Then why did you say management skills?! What are management skills?

Laurie looked like he had much the same question in mind, but glared half-heartedly at Jon and nodded. "Yeah. When I find my management skills. You'll owe me when I find my management skills."

Jon tucked his lute away behind the bar counter and flicked his brother a salute. "Yes, I will. Thanks, bro."

Alis grabbed his hand and dragged him away from the faire.

"THIS IS AMAZING," Alis said half an hour later as they milled around, waiting for the pizzas they'd ordered from a food truck. "Most of the faires I go to aren't quite so close to a town, or it's a much bigger city, so I don't get...*this.*"

She gestured broadly at the streets of midweek-evening Renaissance, Colorado. The sun had fallen behind the mountains, but it was nowhere near dark yet. Everything had that flattering, lingering twilight blue, interrupted by the occasional amber pool of an enthusiastically early street light. Hundreds of people were out in the beautiful evening, waiting in line at restaurants, eating outdoors, sitting on park benches, all happy and chatting.

And fully half of them were in faire garb. There were elves and fairies, princes and princesses, peasants and merchants, all wearing the same clothes they'd had on all day at the faire. On one hand, they were incongruous with the tall flat Old West facades and brick or wood-slatted storefronts. On the other, even that incongruity helped to make the town itself seem enchanted.

Jon nodded. "It's my favorite time of the year. When I was really little the faire wasn't as big, and the costumes weren't as elaborate, but I honestly believed it was magic. Now that I'm older..." He smiled, almost shyly. "Now I'm sure it is."

Emotion welled up in Alis's chest, taking her breath away and bringing stinging tears to her eyes. She pressed her hand over her heart, trying to catch her breath, utterly overwhelmed. "You're right," she said in a small, happy voice. "It is magic. It's all magic. Oh, God, I think I love you."

Her eyes widened and she clapped her hand over her mouth, shocked that the words had fallen from it. She hadn't even *thought* them. They just came with that huge upswell of emotion, a truth that was suddenly so obvious that she'd had to say it.

Jon's shy smile turned incredulous, then hopeful, without losing any of the shyness. "Really?" He sounded as small-voiced and happy as she felt, but less embarrassed, she thought.

Alis nodded, her hand still over her mouth. Then she moved it enough to whisper, "Sorry, I don't know where...that was a lot, I—"

Whatever apology or protest she was trying to offer was muffled by Jon's tender kiss. It drowned all her doubts, making her feel absolutely safe and certain, and when it finally broke, Jon whispered, "I know I'm in love with you. I get that it's complicated, that we've only known each other a few days, but…but yeah, Alis. It's real. Whatever else is going on, whatever else happens, this is real."

"You think love at first sight is a thing?" she asked shakily, then wobbled a smile. "Although I guess it was laugh at first sight, in our case…"

Jon brushed his thumb along her jaw, smiling down at her. "I do think love at first sight is a thing, and if it starts with laughter, it's got to be good, right? What's better than laughing with somebody you love?"

"*Pizza for Jon and Alis!*" somebody inside the pizza truck window bellowed, with such perfect timing that Alis's nerves vanished in a burst of laughter.

"Apparently pizza is."

"Nah, pizza's just the topping on the…" Jon trailed off, looking perplexed. "…on the pizza? You wouldn't want pizza on your ice cream, and pizza *has* toppings, so…"

"Mmm, ice cream. After the pizza, maybe." They got their pizzas and went to pull up a bit of curb, their feet in the street. Alis opened her pizza box, inhaling the scent of sauce, cheese and pepperoni with deep appreciation, then put it down so it could cool enough to eat as she watched people drift back and forth across the street. "Do the streets always roll up at 6pm here? Also, is that *Shelly*?"

She stood up indignantly, looking down the road toward where the woman who was supposed to play Princess Cecilia was leaving a Chinese take-out place with enough food to feed a family of four. "It is. Oh my God. She looks *fine*. And if she's going to eat that much she must not be sick from food poisoning anymore. I swear to God if she's not at the faire tomorrow...!" Alis sat back down, still indignant, and kicked a small rock into the street. "I can't believe she's out here getting... well, anyway. What was I saying?"

"You were asking if the streets always rolled up early. You know, I always thought that phrase meant everything closes at six, but..." Jon waved at the undeniably open-for-business town. "But yeah. It's part of the traffic laws they implemented that the resorts hate. During any kind of festival, vehicular traffic is banned from downtown after six. There's parking at the grocery stores and strip malls, so people can walk in from a few blocks out, but the town runs shuttle buses almost everywhere in a five mile radius during the faire so people don't have to drive."

"You must have the most forward-thinking people on the planet in your town council." Alis sent one more half-hearted glare in Shelly's direction as the woman disappeared in the distance. Then she tried her pizza, which was still too hot, and left it to sit again. "Seriously, how did you get everybody to agree to that?"

Jon tested his own pizza, then took a bite even though it was still steaming like crazy. Then he hissed and breathed through his teeth, trying to cool his mouth. Once he was done burning his tongue, he dropped his voice. "It started out as a way of controlling access to the town for the safety of the shifter population. It just happened that we started trying to put the laws in at the same time a bunch of hippies settled here, and the whole 'people first' thing was very strongly their vibe. So for the past sixty years or so Renaissance has been really…well, these days you'd call it green-oriented, I guess, but it's just trying to be safe for everybody and treat people like they're more important than cars."

"Can you elect a town for President? Because I'd vote for that," Alis said with a shake of her head. "That's really great. I could I—" She broke off sharply that time, because she'd been about to say *I could live in a place like this*, and it was big enough that she had already dropped the L-word unexpectedly. She wasn't quite ready to say she'd think about *moving* to Renaissance.

Although the truth was, Alis already knew in her heart that if one of them was going to move, it was going to be herself. Jon's family business was in Renaissance. Maybe even more importantly, access to the wilderness, which had to be important to a man who could turn into a giant grizzly bear, was here.

She still didn't quite want to say it aloud. Maybe because at the least, she wished there could someday be a discussion about it, instead of taking it for granted that Alis would move. Assuming this new, fragile, shining thing between them worked out at all.

Jon had stopped trying to eat his too-hot pizza and was watching her with a gentle expression. When she finally glanced at him, he said, very softly, "Your life is back East. I wouldn't ask you to just throw that all away because Renaissance is *my* home. My big brother's up in New York, but he's running a brewpub of his own, not out there selling and marketing Thunder Bear's product. If things go well with our expansion, I could go out East, Alis. I could take point on every-thing east of the Mississippi and leave Laurie the western half of the country." He smiled a little. "That's almost enough for him and his ego, anyway."

Alis blurted a little sobbing laugh and leaned in to kiss Jon fiercely. "Are you actually perfect?"

"God, no. I leave my socks all over the house. And I know we're not anything like there yet, but you looked like you needed to hear that I wasn't going to expect you to uproot your whole life for me, if things went that way."

"It was exactly what I needed to hear," Alis said through a tight throat and happy tears. "Does being a shifter come with telepathy, too, or something?"

"Oh my *god* wouldn't that be *cool*? But no, I just try not to be a total dick, you know?"

Alis laughed again, this time lower and more throatily. "I'd say you're zero percent dick but I am *gratefully* aware that's not true."

Jon coughed. "I'd like to think I'm exactly the right percentage dick, yes. Maybe a little bit generously dick, actually."

"Definitely generous." Alis felt herself blushing and grabbed her pizza while Jon grinned into his. Her phone buzzed and she checked it while gnawing on a pizza bone.

A text from Jasmine said *are you ever coming home?*

No, I'm running off to live in a cabin in the woods with Sword Boy. Why?

Just wanted to make sure you're still alive. It's been at least eleven minutes since we've communicated with each other and you know I get nervous when we're apart for more than that long.

Alis laughed, because they'd been born eleven minutes apart. *Love you, baby sis.*

Yeah, I love you too, old lady. Text if you're not coming home AGAIN.

I WIIIILLLLLL. Sorry for being out of touch.

Jasmine sent *it's okay* and the "I GUESS" guy meme, and Alis chuckled as she put her phone away again.

"Everything okay?"

"My sister checking up on me. Apparently she thinks I've joined a cult for some guy and we're forbidden communication with the outside world, or something. We text a lot," she added fondly. "Possibly enough to be weird, I don't know."

"Oh, no. You should see our family chats. Sometimes I'm not sure how people get all the gossip they share, since as far as I can tell it takes twenty-four hours a day, seven days a week just to keep up with it on the chat. I'd like to meet her someday. You said she's still back in Maryland?"

Alis had almost forgotten he didn't know Jasmine was in Renaissance with her to play the part of Lady Alessandra sometimes. Suddenly explaining that felt awkward, although it was going to get worse if she didn't mention it soon.

On the other hand, maybe she could get Jazz to come to the fair when *she* was being Lady Alessandra, too, and they could do some kind of silly French farce thing as their big reveal. Alis smiled at the idea, and shook her head. "No, she's a digital nomad. Works from wherever she wants. She goes to Mexico for the winter, half the time. I swear I chose the wrong profession. Except I hate computer programming."

"Do you like kids?" Jon screwed up his face and sighed at his pizza. "I was trying to *not* make that sound like a loaded question, but I'm not sure that's possible."

"Hah! Yes, I do. I'd be miserable as an elementary school teacher otherwise. And..." Alis leaned her shoulder against his. "Yes, I do. To the loaded part of that question. Oh." She widened her eyes. "Um. Does it, uh, do you, I mean."

"Yes," Jon said, obviously both amused and understanding her. "Usually shifters breed true."

"So we'd have...baby bears..." Alis felt like individual bits of her brain were exploding as she tried to assimilate that information. In fact, she bet it was visible from the outside. There were probably fireworks going off inside her eyes, one at a time. Pew, bang, kerpow. "Wow, that's. That's. Wow."

"I am not planning to rush into that particular minefield any time soon," Jon said firmly. "*If* we get there, it'll be in enough time for you to get used to the idea."

"Wait." Alis took her phone out and checked something. "Wait, so does that mean I'd only have to be pregnant for...how long are bears pregnant for?"

Jon's laugh bounced down the street so loudly a bunch of people nearby turned to look at them before going back to their own conversations. "On one hand I'm sorry to say it doesn't work that way, and on the other I'm sorry to say it's way more complicated than with humans. They have delayed embryo implantation, so—"

"Nope! Nope, stop there, that's enough, I'll do it the human way." Alis turned her attention to a combination of finishing the now-cool-enough pizza and scooting around trying to de-numb her butt, which wasn't fond of sitting on concrete. "Wait, does your butt not get numb? Is that part of the healing-shifting thing?"

"I'm sorry to report that it also doesn't work like *that*. My butt is also numb and if I wanted to de-numb it fast I'd have to shift, which…" Jon waved a piece of pizza at the busy streets. "Probably wouldn't go over well."

"Right, with the running and the screaming." Alis's eyebrows drew down. "How many people here wouldn't run and scream?"

Jon's eyebrows went up as if in response, and he studied the street for a few minutes. "Maybe ten percent? There are quite a few of us out right now."

"And you can tell how?"

"The scent, a little. The look, a little. Mostly it's my bear telling me so."

Alis laughed, startled. "Your bear? What?"

His smile was warm and rueful. "It's a voice in my head. We talk. It encourages me to make rash decisions. When I shift, I'm a voice in *its* head. It's more than coexisting. We're the same being. But we do kind of have separate ideas about things. That sounds schizophrenic, doesn't it?"

Alis shook her head, smiling. "It sounds magical. So

you really would know, or your bear would, if a shifter had been at City Hall."

"We should. It *feels* like one was there. But it's like a blank space where all the information about it should be. It's like..." Jon fell silent, looking thoughtful. "Like having your nose plugged and your eyes covered and then given an apple to eat, except when you can see and smell it you realize it's an onion."

"What?! I can tell an onion from an apple!"

"Okay, bear in mind I haven't actually tried this myself, but, no, apparently you can't. They're supposed to have really similar textures, and since scent and vision are actually a huge part of taste..."

"I'm horrified," Alis said. "I want to try. Except I really, really *don't* want to try. But really?"

"It's what I've read. I could try it. The bear likes onions. Raw or otherwise."

"I am not kissing you after that," Alis said firmly. "But okay, even if I'm skeptical about the whole onion/apple thing, I get your point. Someone's taken away so much information that your mouth thinks it's an apple because it feels like one, but there's evidence it's an onion from the scars on the desk." She squinted. "You know what I mean."

Jon grinned. "Yeah. And you know what I mean. So we're looking for a shifter who can hide who they are," he said with less humor. "And I've never even heard of such a thing."

"Obviously I haven't either. But there must be some way to take the plug off our noses, and remove the blindfold." Alis watched people drift back and forth between businesses, sharing drinks, food, and stories. "If you were going to kidnap somebody around here, where would you bring them?"

"Up the mountain," Jon said with a shrug. "There are a million places you could hide out. Especially if you were a shifter, but even if you weren't. Why?" He cast her a glance. "Are we going to go looking?"

"Well, you could scent out the mayor, at least, right? Or, could you? I don't really know how well bears scent."

"Only a few thousand times better than humans. As opposed to dogs," Jon said when Alis threw him a wry, questioning glance. "Who scent millions of times better than humans."

"What about wolves? Are they on the dog or bear end of things?"

"Dog, definitely."

"Maybe we should ask a wolf, then."

CHAPTER 22

GUS SAUNDERS, the police officer, happened to be a wolf. Jon shot him a text, asking if he was available, and the officer called back a minute later. Jon put him on speakerphone so Alis could hear as Gus said, "If you're thinking of sniffing Whitfield out, I tried."

Jon said, "Dammit," and the officer snorted.

"I *am* good at my job, Jon. Fran said you had a sniff around at Whitfield's place too, and came up with nothing. What are you looking for?"

"Somebody who doesn't smell like an onion," Jon mumbled.

There was a pause in which he could more or less hear Gus mentally translating 'onion' to 'shifter,' and a longer one in which the officer clearly decided not to ask why Jon had settled on *onions* as a code word for shifters, For God's Sake. The 'For God's Sake' part came through pretty clearly, without actually being said.

"All right," Gus said after that pause. "Here's the

weird thing I noticed: even at his house, Whitfield's own scent smelled old. Not a few days old, but old enough to have almost disappeared. Wiped out levels of old. And City Hall smelled the same way. Whatever *onions* they're using, they don't just make it hard to smell other...onions. They also make it hard to smell regular...not-onions."

"Apples," Jon offered, and could once more hear Gus basically staring at him through the phone. He should have made a vone call so he could actually see that look, which he bet was kind of funny.

"All right," Gus said eventually. "They make it hard to smell apples, too. Whatever's going on here, they obviously know about onions and have a way of counteracting them. So if you start noticing people, ah, *apples*, that you can't smell..."

"Right. That's helpful," Jon said. "Thanks, Gus. I'll get friends at the Faire to put their noses into it and I'll let you know if we come up with anything."

"I'm already doing the same around town." Gus hung up without making any promises about sharing *his* information with Jon, but Jon guessed that was fair. He wasn't the one whose job was solving crimes, after all.

Alis had finished her pizza and was smirking at him. "That was the most ridiculous conversation I've ever heard, and I teach eight year olds. Also, I'm calling you guys onions in public forever now, if I have to bring up the whole..." She paused dramatically. "'Onion' thing."

"I can't wait to explain that to my family," Jon said with a groan. "No one is ever going to believe I didn't onion-breath you half to death."

Alis laughed and leaned into him, her head on his shoulder. He put his nose in her hair, inhaling *her* scent, which was still sunshine-warm and sunblocky, with traces of sweat, deodorant, and shampoo. Nothing overpowering, just pleasant. "The good news is *you* smell great. Citrusy?"

"I have an incredible weakness for orange body scrubs," she admitted. "They make me go around sniffing myself all day."

"I volunteer as tribute."

"You can sniff me any time," Alis promised. "Should we go sniff the townsfolk? Not that I'm going to be of any use, with my blunt human nose."

He kissed the arch of her nose, which was anything but blunt. "Hatchets are sharp and deadly. And before you get offended, you were the one who used 'hatchet' to describe yourself in the first place. *I* think you're a classic beauty. Romanesque."

"I'm not offended. I like the idea of being sharp and deadly. And Romanesque isn't exactly the 'in' look for women these days, but I'll take it."

"It's extremely in, in Rome."

"Is it, though?" Alis asked curiously. "Okay, we have to get up, whether it's to sniff people or not. My butt has gone completely to sleep."

"Want me to rub it for you?"

"Not in public!"

Jon made a show of taking notes. "'Private butt rubbing appreciated...'"

"I'll rub *your* butt," Alis said, then shook her head. "That didn't come across as threateningly as I meant for it to. I sound like one of my kids, in fact."

"I'm not sure a good butt-rubbing is ever all that threatening," Jon agreed. They were up and walking along the street now, with part of his mind on trying to scent the people around him. A lot of them smelled like sunburn, really, kind of hot and crinkly. "No pressure, but where am I taking you back to, tonight?"

"Oh..." Alis sounded wistful. "I want to go back to your place, but I really need to be at the fairgrounds early tomorrow. Things are going to be complicated unless Shelly comes back to work."

"Tomorrow's..." Jon ran through the faire schedule, trying to remember. "I've got the unarmored division, and then there's the armored later. Princess Cecilia's supposed to be at both of those, isn't she? But especially the armored one, so she can fall in love with Argent."

"Yes, but I want to cheer for you at the unarmored division," Alis said grumpily. "I'm going to be really frustrated if Shelly doesn't show up. Even if I can make you my champion in the unarmored division, Argent's got both the armored and the jousting rounds."

"It's just a show." Jon paused to lean against a building and tug Alis into his arms, nuzzling down for a kiss. "I'm pretty confident I've got the girl in the real world. Tell you what, I'll bring you back to the fairgrounds tonight and see if I can find some of the other onions and get the word out about scentless apples."

Alis's shoulders shook with amusement as she nestled close. "All right. That sounds okay. I should get a good night's sleep, anyway. Tomorrow is going to be a long day."

CHAPTER 23

SHELLY WASN'T at work in the morning.

Alis wasn't angry, she thought: just disappointed. Except, no, she was angry. She only had a little time with Jon before she had to head out to Seattle, and she didn't want to waste it playing Princess Cecilia to Lord Argent's smarmy arrogance. Especially when she was certain she'd seen Shelly the evening before, picking up Chinese food on Main Street.

"I don't think she was sick at all," she muttered to Jasmine as they got her dressed in Shelly's gown. "I think she's playing hooky."

"It's not that I think you're wrong," Jasmine said, fastening Alis's bodice, "but ren faire actors, especially for these big festivals, are usually pretty serious about their performances. If she's not sick, what would be important enough to make her miss it, that she would also have to lie about? If somebody else was sick, or somebody had died or something, she'd tell the Faire about it. The show must go on, yeah, but there are exceptions."

"Yeah, I don't know." Alis sighed, took a deep breath, and coughed again.

"Too tight?" Jasmine went to loosen her stays, but Alis shook her head.

"Just whatever deodorant or perfume she uses. I don't like it."

Jasmine stuck her nose in Alis's armpit, sniffed, and fought off making a pained face. Her, "I don't think it's too bad," was bright and not very convincing.

"First, you're a terrible liar, and second, you're trying to be reasonable with someone who doesn't want to hear the voice of reason right now."

"Hey! I'm not that bad a liar! But okay, yeah, it kind of stinks and I want you to move far far away from me so I never have to smell it again. Better?"

"Just great, since you're going to have to wear this stupid thing all afternoon. No, actually, I'm glad you also don't like it, because I thought maybe I'd gotten hypersensitive to smells because we've been talking about them so much."

"We have?"

"Jon and I have."

Jasmine stepped back from finishing the dress's bits and bobs to give Alis a funny look. "You two have been talking about how things *smell*? Is this some kind of new swipe right kinda thing?"

"Hah! No, I don't think so. It's just…he has a really acute sense of smell? So we've been talking about it." This was not going to work, Alis realized. She couldn't possibly keep Jon's shifting a secret from her twin sister. She also couldn't possibly betray it without talking to him first, but Jasmine was her *twin*. Alis would never keep a secret that big from her.

Of course, she still had to tell Jon she was the Black Knight, too, so there were all kinds of secrets that needed revealing. She sighed and stepped forward to give her sister a long hug. "I know I was looking forward to getting this far west, but honestly, I think I'll be really glad when this particular faire is over."

"Yeah? What about Sword Boy? Will you be glad to be over him?"

Alis sat abruptly in a fluff of skirts, feeling over-whelmed. "No. No, I'm not sure I'm ever going to get over him. I really like him, Jazz. Like…maybe I'm in love with him, like him." She was certain of it, but also not quite certain enough to say it to a twin who would point out Alis had known Jon for less than a week, and that that was an awfully fast turnaround from 'meet cute' to 'in love.'

To her surprise, Jasmine crouched in front of her and took her hands. "Yeah, I was getting that vibe. Oh, come on, Al. I literally don't remember the last time you blew off our hang-out-after-the-faire nights in the RV. I think it might never have happened before. You obviously really like this guy. And let's be real, I've only talked to him as you—"

"As Lady Alessandra," Alis stressed.

"Okay, as Alessandra, who is definitely not named after the sister named Alis or anything, but sure, what-ever. But he seems really nice. And honestly, I think I'm confusing him. Every time he looks at me it's like he thinks something is wrong. I know we're crazy identical and we do everything we can to play that up at the faires, but I'm pretty sure he knows, Alis. Did you tell him you've got a sister?"

"Yeah." Alis squirmed guiltily. "I told him I had a little sister. But not that she was at the faire."

"I'm only eleven minutes younger than you!"

"Still my little sister."

Jasmine rolled her eyes. "Okay, so maybe he doesn't *know* know, but he knows something's up. You definitely have to tell him."

"Yeah, I just…I kind of want to get through the rest of the tourney. I want to keep the Black Knight for myself just for the rest of this show. I don't know, Jazz." Alis sighed and slumped further, which wasn't easy, in a corset. "I've gotten in the habit of keeping it a secret so long it's really hard to admit to it, even when I want to. And I did try a couple of times! In fact, you interrupted once when you called."

Jasmine grimaced. "Oh. Ooops. Oh! Hah! Was that when you said I had terrible timing, or something?"

"It was!"

"Oh! I thought you were about to get laid!"

"That also would have been terrible timing!"

Jasmine got up and flopped across the opposite chair. "Well, okay. As long as you're going to tell him after the tournament, I guess another couple days won't hurt. But you don't want to make him feel like you've been lying to him, Al."

The second was that nobody on earth, least of all Alis herself, could possibly resist that opportunity. With a huge, shit-eating grin already plastered across her face, she pulled her helmet off, shook her hair loose from the pins that held it in place, and cried, "*But I am no man!*"

CHAPTER 26

JON SAID, "OH, THANK *GOD*," as the crowd around him went ape-shit wild, their cries enough to raise a roof that didn't even exist. People were on their feet, stomping, clapping, *screaming,* as Alis slammed into a thunderstruck Argent, attacking with such vigor that the 'elf lord' fell back, and back again, before even starting to mount a defense.

It was too late by then: Alis had him on the ropes, battering him into submission. Every blow got another scream from the crowd, until it seemed like her sword arm was powered by their excitement. There were women beside Jon in tears, clutching each other and sobbing and screaming into each other's faces and at the fighting ring itself, overjoyed by the Black Knight's incredible, unexpected, reveal.

Jon swayed, as stunned as everyone around him. More stunned. More stunned than anyone except—

He turned toward the stands, where Lady Alessandra had collapsed into her seat, mansprawled like the best of them, her jaw dropped and eyes creased in a huge, body-shaking laugh. Jon couldn't hear it from across the distance, not even if the screams hadn't been so utterly thunderous, but she was visibly, obviously thrilled and delighted beyond words. The court around her was torn, half of them watching the fight and screaming their fool heads off, the other half snapping their gazes back and forth between Lady Alessandra and the Black Knight, her *twin sister.*

You see, his bear said, *I **said** that was your mate.*

You could have been a little clearer about things!!!

The bear felt genuinely injured. *I was perfectly clear!*

Jon spluttered, half mad at the bear, half mad at himself for not figuring it out, half mad at Alis for not telling him, half relieved, half—half something else, too, probably, even if that made up far too many halves.

Alis was just *pounding* on the Silver Knight now, absolutely obliterating him, fighting at a speed she couldn't possibly keep up, with strength beyond human norms. But then, Jon thought, if he had that kind of audience support behind him, if he had just pulled off a reveal of that magnitude, if he had been clever enough to do it on *that line,* he too would have felt able to fight until the end of time. Alis's face shone with a sweaty grin, her sword flying faster and faster until it suddenly darted in, slammed into Lord Argent's sword wrist, and disarmed him with an ease that suggested she'd been toying with him all along.

Argent gaped as his sword flew away, watching it and not Alis. She snagged a foot out, caught his ankles with it, and with a straight-armed thrust, shoved him to the ground. Her sword went to his throat, and for all that it was blunted, a weapon meant for performance instead of killing, the whole audience gasped in unquestioning belief.

Then the screaming began again, just noise, wild, excited noise that gradually became a chant of *Al! Eh! San! Dra! Alessandra! ALESSANDRA!*

For some reason, Jon found tears streaming down his cheeks.

Alis looked up with a wild grin, her gaze locking on his despite the hundreds of people to find him amidst, and she mouthed, *I'm sorry.*

Jon put his hand over his heart, shook his head, and finally began to laugh, the tears still running down his cheeks. He shook his head again, bowed toward her, and then, with laughter and tears and joy, took the favor *her sister* **Jasmine** had tied around his arm, and raised it toward the Black Knight, his fated mate, the woman he loved more than the world itself.

Alis laughed, silent beneath the roars of the crowd but shining in her face as she strode forward to accept the favor. Jon hauled her into a kiss despite the fact she was wearing armor, and somehow the noise around them redoubled. Alis wrapped her free arm around his neck, her favor clutched in her hand, her sword arm twisted out of the way, and returned the kiss with all the passion that he'd been missing.

Something changed in the tenor of the crowd's roar, a note of warning growing in it. Jon hadn't yet really begun to realize it when his bear snarled *Look out!*—

—but Alis knew, Alis was attuned to the audience's

mood, Alis was buoyant on their power, Alis was already turning away, the favor still clutched in her hand as she brought it to her weapon's hilt and changed the blade she'd been using for speed, one-handed, into the bone-breaking power of a two-handed sword.

Many things happened very fast, so fast that time slowed down for them, there in the dusty lists under a relentless blue sky. The first was that Argent swung at Alis; the second was that she ducked beneath his blow, so close that Jon saw his sword brush her hair as it flew up while she ducked down.

The third was how she spun, grace and rage in motion, and rose with the motion so that when her own blade came up, it was into the bottom shoulder joint of Argent's armor. His shoulder dislocating may not have made a sound, but *he* did: a scream that cut through the audience's wild shouting.

The fourth thing, the one that nobody noticed, thank god, was that Laurie, who hadn't even *been* there a second ago, grabbed Jon's shoulders and threw him backward off the fence he was in the process of vaulting, keeping him from shifting into a bear to protect his mate in front of an audience of hundreds.

Jon hit the ground with a groan that had nothing on Lord Argent's. Laurie, standing above him wild-eyed, looked like he didn't know what to do next, and like he thought it was possible Jon would get up and murder him. Instead Jon put his hand up, Laurie pulled him to his feet, and Jon muttered, "Thanks."

Laurie's shoulders slumped in relief as the sound of

metal scraping on metal caught both their attentions. They both turned toward the fighting ring again, where Alis was placing a foot on Argent's chest and crouching like that, all gleaming black metal in the sun. The crowd went wild again, which meant it took a shifter's hearing to catch Alis growling, "Now tell me what the fuck you did with Whitfield before I beat it out of you like the people want me to."

Laurie said, "*What?*" and Jon, gaping, shook his head and surged back toward the fence, trying to hear better. Argent was mumbling, inaudible even to Jon's ears, but after a long moment Alis looked satisfied.

Then she grabbed his left gauntlet, pulled it off his hand, and lifted it to the audience. "See the evidence of Argent's dishonorable actions!" she bellowed. "He fights unfairly in every bout, and I, the Black Knight, *demand* that his honors and accolades be revoked from this and every Faire across the land!"

As she spoke, she discarded her own gauntlet so she could put her hand into Argent's. She pulled something out, then lifted it: a tiny ring light that sputtered, then flashed a violently blinding LED. Alis turned slowly, shooting incredible shards of dazzling brilliance into people's eyes as the crowd's roars turned from confusion to disapproval. When she was certain everyone understood what was going on, Alis stalked to the stands where her sister and the rest of the Red Court sat, and flung the gauntlet down.

"My lords and ladies!" she cried to them. "I stand before you now as my true self, Lady Alessandra, the Black Knight of the Eastern Kingdoms! I beg forgiveness for my deceit these many years, and thank my beloved twin, the Lady Jocelyn, for her assistance in carrying out this charade. It was not shame or fear of rejection that brought me to fight as Lord Edward," she added in audible amusement as she lost hold of her 'Olde English' phrasing for a moment. "It was just you all assumed I must be a man, and I thought I'd see how long it was before anybody figured it out. It took a lot longer than I expected!"

A roar of laughter and applause went up, and Alessandra's name was chanted around the ring for a full minute before she finally turned to the crowd, bowed, and patted it down, a huge smile fixed in place. "Thank you," she called. "Thank you all for embracing my true self. But as you can see, your majesties, I am especially uninterested in wooing either Lady Jocelyn or Princess Cecilia!"

Another laugh rose as Jasmine performed a delicate shudder and Alis grinned wildly, first at her sister, then at the Red King and Queen. "Have I your permission to select my *own* paramour, majesties?"

"God forbid we stand in thy way," the Red King said dryly. "Our hearts do tremble in fear at what lessons we might learn at the tip of thy sword. We prithee, Lady Knight, introduce us to the one who has captured thy heart."

"Armsman!" Alis strode across the field toward Jon, a huge smile still stretching her face. "Cross into the battlegrounds, if you will!"

This time Laurie didn't stop Jon as he vaulted the fencing. Another ridiculously huge roar of approval rose, then reached an impossible crescendo as Alis, in her armor and all, *knelt in front of him* and took his hand. Jon didn't consider himself a man prone to swooning, but he was suddenly in real danger of it as Alis beamed up at him.

"Armsman Jonathan, if you will have me, I pledge my strong sword arm, my honor, and my heart to thee here and now, before all these witnesses. Wilt thou in exchange consent to be my best beloved, my minstrel, my merchant, master of my heart?"

"Holy shit, dude," Laurie whispered from the other side of the fence, "I think you just got proposed to."

Jon, dizzy with astonishment, was pretty sure he had, too. His voice cracked as he said, "I accept your pledge and give my consent," and then, realizing nobody could possibly have heard him under all the screaming, nodded to make sure they all knew he'd said yes.

He hadn't known it was possible for people to make that much noise as Alis stood, wrapped her armored arm around his neck again, and kissed him breathless. Against his mouth, she murmured, "Sorry for putting you on the spot. It seemed like a good idea at the time."

"It was the best idea in the history of the world," Jon whispered back. "What the hell is going on with Argent?"

"Hopefully right now the medics are taking him away," she breathed, which happened to be what was, in fact, going on. "But I finally realized, Jon. He smells weird to *me*."

Jon's eyes widened, but before he could say

anything else, Alis added, "I have to introduce you to the King and Queen," and grabbed his hand, dragging him over to the royal stands. "Majesties, may I introduce you to Armsman Jonathan Brewster, master of the unarmored sword division and the only man to ever conquer my heart?"

"We cannot have this," the king said in deep, disapproving tones as the crowd died down to hear what they were saying. Died down for a moment: a massive protest arose at what he *did* say, until the king glared it into silence again. "We cannot have our most noble knight, known throughout all of these lands as honorable, above reproach and ranked, too, as a lady of our court, beloved to a commoner. Kneel, Jonathan."

Jon, dizzy with nerves all over again, did as he was told to the rising cheers of the crowd again. The king stepped down from the royal stands, put a hand out, and accepted Alis's sword into it before touching Jon's shoulders, once, twice, thrice. "Arise, Jonathan Brewster, Lord and Knight, and be welcome into the Red Court!"

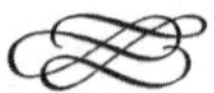

IT TOOK…A *while*…to extract herself from the legions of adoring fans, after that. Alis hadn't anticipated that, and Jon, who was apparently not at all threatened by his girlfriend being the premiere knight in the realm, sat back and grinned at it all. Women and girls, young and old, kept coming up and crying on Alis, and then she would cry on them, and by the time Jon helped her get away, Alis was headachy and dehydrated, but as joyful as she could ever remember being.

"I'm so sorry," she said as soon as she got the chance. "I should have told you I was the Black Knight, but every time I started to, something came up."

"You have no idea what I've been going through." For some reason Jon didn't seem at all upset. "First—all right, first, do you want to get out of that armor?"

Alis felt an unexpected swell of pride and embarrassment rise up in her. "Kind of no? This is the first time I've ever gotten to be *me* in it, although it might make us talking kind of difficult," she added as more women came up to congratulate her.

It took well over an hour to make it back to Jon's tavern, but every slow step of the way was so worth it. Jon simultaneously hung back to let Alis have her moment, but was always *there*, keeping an eye on her, making her feel supported, and somehow not twitching with agitation to find out everything she had to tell him.

When they finally got back to the tavern, enough people wanted to buy Alis drinks that she had to hand them out to others, or she'd be too drunk to breathe, never mind talk, walk, or think. So it was nearly closing time before she and Jon finally sat down in the warm, pine-scented air to duck their heads together and, as it turned out, both start talking at the same time.

Jon said, "The thing about the Black Knight is," as Alis said, "I did want to tell you about being Lord Edward—" before they both broke into laughter and went through a round of protesting, "You go first, no, no, *you* go first," until Alis lifted her hands and said, very firmly, "You first."

As if he'd been bursting to say it, Jon blurted, "The thing I didn't tell you yet about shifters is that we know when we've met the person we're meant to be with forever. That's why I was so sure about us last night when you said you loved me. I know it's real. But Alis... I saw you, and I knew it was you. And then I saw Lord Edward, and I knew it was *him*. I've never been into guys, so the *shock* of that...! And then your sister...!"

Alis's eyes widened and she clapped her hands over her cheeks. "Oh. Oh no! Oh my God! So sometimes you saw Lady Alessandra and it was me and everything was good and sometimes it was Jazz and everything was—"

"*Bad,*" Jon said desperately. "She's obviously very beautiful and everything—you didn't tell me you were twins!—but she wasn't *you,* but I didn't know she wasn't you because you didn't tell me you were twins! So I thought maybe I had to choose between you and Lord Edward, but I could never find him to talk to him, and every time I saw two out of three of you my bear said 'that's our mate' and then the third person it was like 'nah brah' and—" He put his face in his hands, too, then looked up through his fingers, helpless with laughter and relief. "Five hundred people were out there screaming their heads off when you removed your helmet and I was just like 'oh thank GOD.'"

Alis leaned over the table to kiss him thoroughly. "I couldn't tell you Jazz was my twin without blowing the whole Black Knight thing, but I swear, Jon, I was going to tell you as soon as the tourney was over. Although I don't even know what's going to happen with that now," she realized in the moment. "Argent was supposed to compete in the jousting."

"Someone will take his place," Jon said carelessly, "but what *about* Argent, what was that—how did you—?"

She held her hands up, smiling wildly. "I don't know everything. I don't think I know everything, anyway. But do you remember Shelly's perfume?"

Jon rolled his eyes, obviously trying to come up

with a scent, then shook his head. Alis shrieked and threw her hands upward. "Really? Smells like a skunk rolled in roses?"

"Ew. No, I'd remember that."

"See, if I'd known that three days ago we might have figured this all out. I don't know what it is about it, Jon, but it does something to shifter body chemistry, or to your noses. Maybe you just can't smell it at all. She must have spent ages working it out. It stinks to high heaven on humans, but that's what was tricking you, I think. Argent was wearing it, and even I could tell there was something weird and wrong with his scent. But that was after I'd called Officer Saunders to check in on Shelly, because if she was wearing this stuff, either she was a shifter or she was working with one, and I thought she might have Mayor Whitfield and that's why she was taking time off from Faire."

The words tumbled out, and Jon's eyes got bigger all the way through. "*And*?"

"And I don't know! I haven't heard from Gus yet!"

"You have now," the officer said, walking up to the table. "I might just take one of those beers, if you don't mind."

Alis straightened like she'd been electrified. "Please do. Did you find Mayor Whitfield?"

"Tied up in Shelly Banks's basement," Gus said with a nod. "Did you know the old guy was a Marine, Jon?"

Jon's eyebrows flew upward. "No I did not."

"As it turns out, neither did Nelson Moore, aka Lord Argent." Gus took a long sip of beer and put the bottle down again, gazing into it before glancing up at

Alis. "You probably saved his life. They'd just about decided to kill him, after spending the last few days arguing about it. It was a stupid plan," he said with a sigh. "From start to finish. But Moore thought he was on to something, and he knew Shelly from some Faires she's been to back East, so he roped her in."

Alis, fairly dancing with agitation, said, "But what *was* the plan?"

"There *are* some people looking to buy up a trade-mark on the 'Renaissance Faire' name," Gus confirmed. "Moore knows a few of them and got early word about it. He thought he could turn a fat profit if he could get hold of the Renaissance, Colorado fairgrounds."

"So why didn't he just buy it?" Jon said, then shook his head and answered his own question. "Because it cost a lot more money than he had, obviously."

"Obviously," Gus agreed. "So he hatched this stupid plan to try to make some kind of land grab. But that's not even the dumbest part." He waited a suitable beat while Alis reached out to grab Jon's hand in anticipation. "The dumbest part is that he specifically wanted to do this to get one over on the Torbens."

Alis froze, then shot a quick look at Jon, seeing if he understood. He shook his head and opened his free hand toward Gus in question.

"Apparently," the officer said, "your brother broke his nose in a tournament fight a couple years ago?"

Jon did a full-fledged double-take, from Gus to Laurie and back again. "He did this because Laurie broke his *nose*? The mayor almost got killed over a *broken nose*?"

"Looks like," Gus said with a disbelieving shake of his head. "He's been nursing a grudge ever since. He was planning to face Laurie in combat here. It was evidently going to make his victory complete: beat Laurie on the battleground, then yank the whole faire away from Renaissance and your family in particular."

"Wow," Alis breathed after a moment. "That guy needs to get out more."

"Well, that's not going to happen," Saunders said dryly. "He's almost certainly going to jail for a long time."

Alis leaned in, lowering her voice. "Do shifters go to true human prisons?"

"Yeah, although with ones like him, we might have to make other arrangements." Saunders dropped his voice, too. "He's a silver fox, and foxes run comparatively small. They can get out of places humans might not be able to."

Jon looked at his hand, making a claw of it. "Then how'd he mark up the desk like that? Even shifter foxes *aren't* that big. How'd they make such a *mess* of City Hall?"

Gus puffed his cheeks out. "Whitfield put up a hell of a fight. Moore says he caused most of the destruction." A grin flashed across the officer's face. "He didn't say it in so many words, but I got the impression the old guy had Moore running scared with his tail between his legs. Apparently he had a shotgun in his office and took a couple shots. I haven't looked into it yet, but it might be that scarring is from pellets."

"It didn't smell like gunpowder," Jon said stubbornly.

Alis squeezed his hand. "But nothing else smelled right, either. I didn't notice pellets buried in the floor, but there was a lot of crap on the floor."

Jon stared at her briefly, then groaned. "Apples and onions. Dammit. I got fixated on the idea those scars were claw marks, and… well, hell. But…" He shook his head, slow delight crawling into his confused smile. "Not gonna lie, I love the idea of Whitfield up there shooting down at Argent, but wouldn't somebody have heard it?"

"How many businesses close up early on the first Friday of Faire?" Gus countered, and Jon groaned again.

"Right. Yeah. Okay. Basically all of them. Which was why he figured he could try this at all. And that's an old building with thick walls and doors. With the door closed, somebody might have just thought it was a car backfiring."

Gus nodded. "A perfect storm. And he would've gotten away with it, too, if it weren't for you meddling kids."

Alis laughed. "No, he wouldn't have. The bank was already dragging its feet over that weird sales release memo."

"Well, true enough. But Whitfield might have ended up dead, and that would have been a shame. Also." Gus's eyebrows flickered up. "He knows about shifters now, so he's probably going to be an even better mayor than he was."

"Jesus, and I thought I was surprised," Alis said. "Can you imagine fighting back during an abduction and finding out your kidnapper can turn into a fox?"

"It's probably a little more surprising than finding out the notorious Black Knight, also known as Lord Edward, is a woman." Gus grinned at her. "Congratulations on your win today, Lady Alessandra. On *all* your wins." He finished his beer, rose, and left them alone while Alis blushed happily, then suddenly grabbed Jon's hand again.

"Oh. Oh, I've got to introduce you to Jasmine, I mean for real, but also, Jon, can I tell her about you? About shifters? Because there's no way I can not. We share everything."

Jon, very primly, said, "I hope you don't share *everything*," and Alis laughed.

"No. No, absolutely not. Okay, almost everything. But this is important," she said more softly. "It would mess up our relationship if I didn't tell her, so I can't not."

"I wouldn't ask you to. She's your twin. I trust her, just like I trust you."

Alis relaxed. "Okay. Okay, thank you. Do you want to meet her?"

"Of course I do." He glanced around. "Is she lurking?"

"I actually think she's down at the Red Court, *holding* court. I kind of shoved her right into the spotlight today."

"Alis, you shoved everybody into the spotlight today, yourself most of all. That was one of the hottest things I'd ever seen. I genuinely thought the entire stadium was losing its mind. You couldn't have planned it better."

"That was when I was absolutely sure, though, you know? He said 'no man' and I thought, you tricksy shifter bastard. But then he also opened the door with that line, and I would have been an idiot to not walk right through. I'm many things," Alis said with satisfaction. "A knight. A girlfriend. A lady fair. But an idiot, I'm not."

Jon started smiling again, slow and hopeful. "A girlfriend?"

"Oh, that's the one you pick up on?"

"Yes. Yes, it is. C'mere." He tugged her to her feet and around the table, into his lap. "Hello, girlfriend."

"Hey, boyfriend. Just for the record, I'm not clear yet on how we're going to make it all work."

Jon stole a kiss. "Don't worry. We will. Fate has it in for us, you know."

"'Has it in for us,'" Alis echoed, amused. "You know that phrase usually means something bad, right?"

"Yeah, but not in this case. In this case, I promise it means amazing things are ahead of us."

"Well, then, let's get started." Alis paused. "As soon as you meet Jasmine. And the rest of my family."

"And my parents. Since you already met half my family anyway. And—" Jon broke off, grinning. "No, wait, we can get *started* before all that. That's what comes next, not the barrier to getting started. Right?"

"Right. In fact, we already have started. Oh my

God." Alis hid her face in Jon's shoulder a moment. "We're overthinking this, right?"

"Yeah." Jon nuzzled her head up until he could kiss her again, and whispered, "Yes, we are. All that matters, Alis, is we've got our happily ever after. Let's just live it, however it works out."

"That sounds perfect," Alis breathed, and it was.

EPILOGUE

EIGHTEEN MONTHS LATER, GIVE OR TAKE

VIRTUE, New York, was *cute*. Picture-book cute. Exactly like Renaissance, Colorado, except completely different. They were both towns that had worked hard to retain their Old Americana charm, but in Virtue that was New England picturesque where Renaissance had the Old West thing going on.

Alis, standing at the corner of the world's most ridiculously large town square, said, "I see why Steve likes it here."

Jon scooted up behind her, wrapping his arms around her like she would freeze otherwise, and nodded over her head. "I'd miss the mountains, but it's a great little town. And the town square is nuts."

It *was*. It had to be several acres in size, although

truthfully Alis was always a little surprised at how small an acre actually was. Still, it was currently filled with Christmas market kiosks and the most enormous Christmas tree she'd ever seen. It sprouted from a gazebo large enough to comfortably house a family of four, if that family didn't mind a little weather getting in on them. Or a lot of weather, really: it was currently snowing like mad, adding to the winter wonderland snow globe vibe the little town already had. People were out shopping, though, all bundled up against the cold. Watching them stomp around, shouting hellos at each other through fuzzy hats and big coats, Alis wondered just how many of them would be more comfortable in their own personal fur coats and big-pawed feet.

Lots, she guessed. Virtue was apparently full of shifters. But in this case, she knew for a fact that at least two dozen of them would be happy to do just that, because more or less the entire Torben clan had descended upon Virtue this year for Christmas.

Well, technically speaking, they'd descended on Jon's second-oldest brother, Steve, his wife Charlee, and, most importantly of all, the adorable, tiny baby girl Charlee had given birth to just six weeks earlier. Amelia Rose was the star of this year's Christmas, and everyone had come to meet her.

'Everyone,' in this case, also included Alis's family: her parents had driven up from Maryland, and Jasmine had, with a great deal of theatrical protestation, flown back home from wintering in Mexico. She had a tan and sun-bleached strands in her dark hair, which made telling her and Alis apart relatively easy for the first time in their lives. She kept muttering about the cold, and although she'd gotten a cider and a hot chocolate while they were walking around the Christmas market, she had also just abandoned Alis and Jon for a doughnut shop that somebody said had great coffee.

Alis's parents had barely left Steve's brewpub, the *Hold My Bear*, where they were alternating between cooing over Amelia Rose and worshipping Charlee herself for her cooking. Alis was fairly certain they'd forgotten about their own biological children entirely, but that was okay: she wasn't quite ready for kids, and if Steve and Charlee's baby filled that void for Alis's parents, more power to them.

Virtue looked like a spectacularly good town to raise a kid in, though. Aside from the assumption that Amelia Rose would grow up safely as a shifter in this town, the square featured a fabulously huge play-ground that was part pirate ship, part treehouse, part jungle gym, and clearly all fun. Even with its wooden frame half-hidden in snow, a couple dozen kids were clambering over it, playing tag, falling down slides, screaming with the effortlessly loud enthusiasm of children everywhere.

"It's good, isn't it?" a kid asked from just down the sidewalk.

"It's amazing," Alis replied. "I'm a teacher and I'd love to have something like this at our school."

"You should talk to my dad." The child walked over, offering a hand to shake. He was about eleven, blue-eyed and pink-cheeked in the cold, with his winter jacket unzipped and his hair matted like he'd *been* wearing a hat, but had convinced it to go elsewhere. "I'm Noah Brannigan. My dad designed it for me. Well, us." He waved airily at the kids at the behemoth playground.

"Oh yeah, Noah!" Jon laughed and shook Noah's hand. "I'm Jon Torben. I know about you. My brother says you're in charge of this town. He owns *Hold My Bear.*"

"Oh, Chef Charlee's husband." Noah nodded approvingly. "Welcome to Virtue. If you need to know anything, just go ahead and ask me. I know everything here."

Alis coughed trying to muffle a laugh and ended up failing. She'd had kids like Noah in her classes: confident, open, and comfortable in practically any setting. They were often inadvertent troublemakers, but she loved them. "Right now I think Steve and Charlee are answering most of our questions, but we'll keep you in mind. It's nice to meet you, Noah. I'm Alis," she added.

Noah eyed her. "You're a school teacher? So your name is probably *Ms* Alis, right?"

"Ms Capellas, in my official capacity. You may call me that, if you like."

"It's very nice to meet you, Ms Capellas." Noah shook her hand, too, looking quite solemn and grown-up about it all. "I hope you enjoy your stay in Virtue." He nodded at Jon, then, suddenly reverting to a little kid, went tearing off toward the playground yelling for a friend of his.

Alis laughed. "If that's the kind of kid this town is producing, Amelia Rose is going to be amazing."

"She's going to be amazing anyway!"

"Well, obviously, but you know what I mean." Alis tucked her arm through Jon's and looked around for her sister. "It's not that big a town. I can't have lost her already."

"She's still in the doughnut shop." Jon turned them around to face the cheerfully glowing storefront and pointed out Jasmine, who was inside with a cup of coffee, a doughnut, and a dippy grin as she talked to a red-headed man. "See, in there flirting with the locals, that's all."

"Well, in that case, we should definitely interrupt her. No, wait, the other thing, we should leave her alone. Right?" Alis grinned up at her husband. "Or we could abandon her and go back to the brewpub to eat delicious food and admire our new niece."

"That sounds like more fun," Jon said. "Better yet, we could go back to the hotel and *practice*," he said with a great deal of emphasis on the word, "making one of our own."

"Oh yes. Practice. We need lots and lots of practice. Let's do that." Alis eyed the town square. "Of course, that means getting to the other side of town without running into any of our relatives, who will undoubtedly want us to come back to the brewpub and have more family time."

"This *is* family time," Jon said firmly, and led her off through town to have his wicked, wonderful way with her.

ACKNOWLEDGMENTS

THANK YOU to so many of my Patreons and early readers, who found some hysterical mistakes in this book before it went to print (thank goodness). Particular thanks to Nicole, Sharon Corbet, Linda Cox, Kate Sherry, TripTripTrip, Mary Hargrove, Carol Guess, Michael Bernardi, Gemma Tapscott, Kathy Rogers, Sarah Brooks, Larisa LaBrant, Sherry, Susan Bauer, Rachel, Doreen Farrer, Tal S, Dónal Cunningham, and Alex McKenzie! You're all my heroes!

Some say Murphy Lawless is the descendant of Irish gangsters, exiled to Australia, who has made good on the family name. It's probably true*.

But then, others claim that Murphy was a spy for the Allies during the war. Stories are told of daring rescues of intrepid reporters from almost certain death, but Murphy has never admitted to anything. Still others say Lawless studied with a local tribe for years after crash-landing in the untamed wilds, having accepted a dare from a pilot of ill repute, and came away from the experience a kinder, wiser, gentler soul.

Even now, though, the most widely held belief is that Lawless left Australia as a mere slip of a thing, and made a fortune in the wilds of the Alaskan oil fields before realizing that romance was the ultimate adventure. Murphy now writes passionate, fun-filled stories of paranormal romance and destined love.

*Probably.

You can find Murphy at CatieMurphy.com, Patreon, and at her newsletter, which is by far the best way to have up-to-date information delivered straight to you!